④

SUSAN SAND
MYSTERY STORIES
THE RIDDLE OF
RAGGEDROCK RIDGE

④ SUSAN SAND
MYSTERY STORIES
THE RIDDLE OF RAGGEDROCK RIDGE
MARILYN EZZELL

PINNACLE   NEW YORK

Susan Sand Mystery #4: The Riddle of Raggedrock Ridge

Copyright © 1982 by Marilyn Ezzell

An original Pinnacle Books edition, published for the first time anywhere.

First printing, October 1982

ISBN: 0-523-41743-8
Cover and illustrations in text by Hector Garrido

Printed in the United States of America

PINNACLE BOOKS, INC.
1430 Broadway New York 10018
New York, New York 10018

To Ann Harriet Leonard
an intrepid friend and Susan's first fan

Contents

Chapter 1

Earth Tremor

"LOOK, SUSAN SAND!" cried Marge Halloran. "Those jagged rocks must be Raggedrock Ridge! Does this riding trail lead all the way up there?"

"I think it goes very nearly to the top," replied Susan Sand, rising in her saddle and shading her eyes from the afternoon sun as she peered through her glasses at the famous mountain. "The groom at the riding stables said the horses would be able to take us to the summit. The incline seems gradual and this trail has certainly been used for many years. The horses are apparently well acquainted with the terrain."

Susan Sand, the renowned mystery story author, and her friend, plump, red-haired Marge Halloran, were on a brief vacation, staying in the town of Foxboro where Susan was engaged in research for her next book. Raggedrock Ridge, located several miles outside the tiny town, was a great attraction for horseback riders, and the girls had decided to spend a day looking over the area.

"I haven't ridden a horse since last summer," said Marge, shifting in the saddle and patting the chestnut mare affectionately. "I feel like a cowgirl!"

"It's fun, isn't it!" rejoined Susan Sand, brushing a strand of raven hair from her forehead. "I think I like the fall best of all the seasons."

"There's a nip in the air," replied Marge. "Soon it will be Halloween. Let's plan a party when we get back to Thornewood."

"That's a grand idea, Marge," agreed Susan. "We can invite Brian Lorenzo, Christine Sommers and Pierre Bernet, and, of course, Professor Randall Scott."

"It seems to me that you put the most important person last, Sue," said Marge in a teasing tone. "I don't think that you ever really forget about Professor Scott."

"I could say the same about you and Brian," returned Susan, wrinkling up her nose and grimacing at her friend. "Didn't we have a wonderful time at Owl Lake last summer."

"Wonderful and exciting!" said Marge, recalling the events of that vacation near Witchwhistle Well nostalgically. "Once you got us involved with Baron Sean and Brenda the Snake Person we had no time to take it easy! Now that I think back, I can hardly believe that it all really happened. That was quite a write-up in the newspaper about you, Sue. Why, you're more famous than ever, both as an author and as a detective."

"If I remember correctly, we were all mentioned in that article," replied Susan, gently urging her black mare along the rocky trail. There was even an article in *The New York Times.*"

"I bet your next book, *The Invisible Mirror,* will be another best-seller!" exclaimed Marge. "Now everyone knows that you are a great detective as well as a first-rate author!"

"Stop!" cried Susan Sand. "'You'll give me a swelled head! I'm just glad that you were able to come along on this research trip, Marge. Foxboro is a charming little town and this territory is a perfect setting for a mystery story. Look how spooky Raggedrock Ridge looks!"

"Isn't there some legend connected with the Ridge?" asked Marge. "It seems to me that . . ."

All at once the ground beneath the two horses seemed to shift and rocks of various sizes started to tumble down from the ridge above. The entire area began to quiver and in another second Marge's horse bolted, throwing the girl to the ground.

"It must be an earthquake!" shouted Susan, pulling hard on the reins in order to control her terrified mare. "The ground is moving!"

For several moments the earth continued to tremble, then, just as suddenly as it had started, the tremor was over. After calming her horse, Susan dismounted and hurried over to where Marge was lying. Marge's horse, which had raced off in panic, was now standing several hundred feet away, dazed.

"Marge, you're hurt!" exclaimed Susan, bend-ing over her friend. "I think it was just an earth tremor. It seems to be over."

"I've hurt my ankle," said Marge, sitting up and rubbing her left leg cautiously.

"Let me look at it," replied Susan. "But I have to take your boot off."

Gently, Susan Sand removed Marge's boot and examined her ankle.

"It's beginning to swell," said Susan, holding the foot in her lap.

"The pain is pretty bad," replied Marge, biting her lip. "Oh, I hope it isn't broken!"

"We must get you to a doctor," Susan Sand stated firmly. "It has to be X-rayed immediately. I'm quite certain that I saw a sign half a mile or so back down the mountain just before the beginning of the trail."

"There was a sign at that Victorian house," Marge recalled. "Dr. Coram, I think it said. But how can I get back there?"

"I'll bind your ankle with my scarf and get you on your horse with your ankle supported," explained Susan, pulling off the green and white neckerchief from around her neck. "If there are no more tremors we should be able to keep the horses at a slow pace."

Soon Susan Sand had tightly wrapped her friend's ankle, and had helped Marge mount the mare. Marge, riding sidesaddle, was able to support her injured ankle in the shortened stirrup just enough to ease the pain.

"I know the house is not far," said Susan comfortingly, riding beside her friend. "Once we reach the beginning of the trail, we should see it around the bend."

In a very short time the girls had made their way back down the trail and were on the main road that led to Foxboro. Within moments a large house appeared, situated on a small rise. A few scraggly trees in the rocky ground gave the property a desolate appearance.

"What an odd-looking house," said Susan. "It's all gables and chimneys with a tower right in the middle."

"There's the sign," commented Marge. "DUDLEY CORAM, M.D. I guess I'm lucky to find a doctor so close."

"Let's hope that he's in," replied Susan, as the horses started up the winding drive that led to the front entrance.

The house was very old, extravagantly Victorian in design, and it appeared to lean toward one side as if years of sitting on the little hill buffeted by the winds that blew down from Raggedrock Ridge had caused it to become part of the landscape.

"I can almost see the carriages drawing up and the footman coming down the steps to usher the guests in," said Susan, her imaginative mind conjuring up a style of living that was long gone.

Just as the girls reached the front door, it opened and a man with a black moustache, dressed in a dark suit, came toward them, smiling.

"What seems to be the matter?" he asked genially. "We don't often have visitors arriving on horseback."

"My friend's horse bolted during the earth tremor. She was thrown and has injured her ankle," Susan replied. "Are you Dr. Coram?"

"Dudley Coram at your service," he replied, bowing rather grandly and approaching Marge's horse. He was a big man, about forty-five years old, broad-shouldered and burly with a ruddy complexion.

"Well, young lady," he said, removing the scarf and running expert fingers over Marge's ankle. "We'll have to get you inside and X-ray this. I don't think it's broken, but an X-ray is in order to be on the safe side."

"I'm surprised you have the equipment out here in the country," Susan stated.

"The nearest hospital is twenty-five miles away, young lady," returned the doctor in an authoritative manner, turning piercing blue eyes on Susan. "It is necessary to be well equipped when one is so isolated. I consider Dudley House a small hospital in itself, old-fashioned though it may seem. And what, may I ask, is your name?"

"Susan Sand," said Susan. "And this is Marge Halloran."

"Not Susan Sand, the mystery story writer?" Dr. Coram queried.

"Yes, Doctor," Susan returned. "In fact, that is

why we are in the area. I am doing research for my next book."

"I am honored to meet you, Miss Sand," he replied, shaking her hand vigorously, "I have enjoyed your books tremendously, especially your last, *The Walking Footprint*."

Susan acknowledged Dr. Coram's praise graciously and helped him carry Marge into the house. The horses were led to the Dudley Stables behind the house by a young man who worked for Dr. Coram.

Entering Dudley House, Susan Sand was again struck by the atmosphere of a past era. Dark wood paneled the foyer, and a large lantern, obviously an antique, stood on a table to the left of the door. The inside of the house was immense, and a long hallway ran to the back where the doctor had his office and consulting room. As Susan and Dr. Coram carried Marge into the room where the X-ray equipment was, a red-haired girl, about sixteen years old with a pale, serious face, came through a nearby door.

"This is my daughter, Penelope," said Dr. Coram. "Pen, this is Susan Sand, the mystery story writer, and her friend, Marge Halloran. Marge's horse bolted during that earth tremor and she was thrown, injuring her ankle."

"Oh, I'm sorry," Penelope replied in genuine concern. "Just when you must have been enjoying your ride. Where did it happen?"

"We were on our way up to Raggedrock Ridge," Marge explained, taking an immediate liking to the girl. "I'm lucky that your house is so close. I don't know what we would have done otherwise."

"We are somewhat isolated out here," Penelope replied. "But father has a lot of patients. They come from all over. Usually Julia Leck, the nurse, is here, but on Saturday afternoon she is off duty. I often help out in emergencies."

Soon the injured ankle was X-rayed, with Penelope Coram assisting efficiently, even to the point of developing the film. Marge breathed a sign of relief when Dr. Coram read the print and announced that no bones were broken.

"We have never had a tremor like this before that I can remember," Penelope stated, expertly binding up Marge's foot with an elastic bandage. "I'll have to tell you the tale about the earthquake that caused Raggedrock Ridge to be formed. But first we must get you into the living room where you will be more comfortable."

"I don't think that the girls will be interested in an old country yarn," said Dr. Coram in a somewhat intimidating manner. "That old tale is a lot of nonsense."

"But, Father, even Mr. Sutter believes that there is some truth to it and the Sutter jewels have never been found so—"

"The Sutter jewels disappeared eighty years ago," her father interrupted. "No one is going to find them now."

"Nevertheless, Father," Penelope replied, "since Miss Sand is a detective as well as an author, I'm certain that she would find the story interesting."

Before anything further could be said, another door opened, and a small, attractive woman, dressed in riding clothes, entered and came down the hall.

"This is Esther Greenway," said Penelope. "Miss Greenway, this is Susan Sand and Marge Halloran. Marge sprained her ankle during the earth tremor when her horse bolted."

"I'm glad that it was just a sprain," replied Miss Greenway. "I was just about to prepare dinner. I hope you girls can stay and have something to eat."

"How kind of you," Susan returned. "We consider ourselves fortunate to have found Dr. Coram just when we needed him."

"We don't usually have emergencies happening so close by," Miss Greenway answered, smiling. "And it's nice for Penelope to have two people near her own age. I sometimes think that she gets lonesome."

"Oh, it would be wonderful if you could stay overnight," Penelope said enthusiastically. "Your horses will be well taken care of in our stables, and we have so much room in the house that part of it is never used. Father, let's have them as guests."

"Certainly, if you would care to stay, you are welcome," Dr. Coram said cordially.

Some time later, after a delicious meal, the small group was seated comfortably in the spacious, ornately decorated living room sipping coffee and enjoying chocolate cake. Susan was not certain what Esther Greenway's position was, but she seemed to be more than a house-keeper and was obviously very close to Penelope. Penelope and Marge felt an immediate rapport and were chatting like old friends.

"Please, tell us about the earthquake that happened long ago," Marge urged. "And everything connected with it."

Susan Sand noticed that Dr. Coram started to say something but checked himself and began to stroke his black moustache. His blue eyes glanced quickly at Esther Greenway and then back to his daughter, but he remained silent.

"It's a long story," Penelope Coram began, her eyes shining. "It involves the Sutter jewels and a possible kidnapping. The Sutter Mansion is not far from here on the other side of Raggedrock Ridge. Arthur Sutter still lives in the house. He is one of Father's patients."

Night had fallen as Susan Sand sat and listened to Penelope excitedly begin the tale. Suddenly the young author was distracted by a movement at the window near where she was sitting. Although long red velvet drapes covered the panes, a small gap remained where the curtains were not completely pulled together against the darkness outside.

Susan turned her head slightly, and to her amazement a face was staring in at the little group seated around the marble mantelpiece where a fire blazed. The face was that of an old woman, so old that it seemed to be nothing but a mass of wrinkles. Dark eyes searched Susan's face, and the girl immediately felt sympathy toward the old woman. For a moment the eyes turned on Penelope. Then the old wrinkled features again turned to Susan. A second later the windowpane was blank. The face was gone.

Chapter II

The Earthquake

INTUITIVELY, Susan Sand did not reveal what she had witnessed through the gap in the drapes. She was certain that no one else had seen the old woman staring in at them. Esther Greenway, Marge, and Dr. Coram were looking at Penelope as she continued her tale of the earthquake on Raggedrock Ridge eighty years before. Was it possible that the old woman was a member of the household and that her mind was unbalanced?

"She seemed to be an outsider yet she was keenly interested in Penelope," Susan told herself. "I think she knows the girl. And I had the definite feeling that she wanted to communicate with me."

"Susan, isn't that exciting?" said Marge, interrupting Susan's musing. "The Sutter jewels were lost eighty years ago and no one knows what happened to them."

"The Sutter jewels?" Susan answered. "Lost during the earthquake?"

"Susan Sand, I don't think that you have been listening to Penelope!" Marge chided. "I bet you're thinking about your next book!"

"Please excuse my rudeness," Susan replied. "I'm afraid my mind was wandering. But I am really very interested."

"The jewels were very famous at the time," continued Penelope. "They had been brought back from India by Bradley Sutter. When the earthquake happened, Quentin Sutter had reached the summit of Raggedrock Ridge, where he was killed. Some people thought that he had been carrying the jewels, but no one knew why and they were never found. When the terrible quake happened, Quentin's cloak got caught between two huge boulders. As he tried to escape, the cloak was torn and part of it remained between the boulders. Later, the local folk, noticing the jagged rocks that had been formed by the shaking of the earth, called the ridge Raggedrock."

"What a frightening story!" exclaimed Marge. "But why would Quentin Sutter have been carrying such valuable gems?"

"There was never any certainty that he was carrying them," returned Dr. Coram, frowning. "The entire tale has no basis in fact. There were many people killed during that earthquake, including two servants here at Dudley House. Afterwards, before order could be established, there was looting and some of the houses were broken into. The Sutter jewels must have been taken at that time."

"Yes, Father, that is a possibility," Penelope replied. "But you must admit that there is a mystery connected with Christopher Sutter, Quentin's baby son. The baby disappeared at the time and was never found."

"The baby Christopher most probably was killed in that earthquake," Dr. Coram said. "There was terrible destruction. In a case like this no one can say what is legend and what is fact."

"It's an interesting story, Dr. Coram," Susan Sand replied, her curiosity aroused. "I would like to know more about the remaining Sutter."

"Arthur Sutter is the only surviving member of a once large family," Esther Greenway answered. "The Sutter Mansion is on the other side of the ridge. The property is not kept up as it once was, but Arthur loves his old house and there is a great deal of wooded area that belongs to him."

"What does he think about the story?" Marge asked.

"He doesn't know any more than anyone else, Marge," Miss Greenway stated. "It all occurred so long ago."

"It's too long ago to be wasting time talking about it," Dr. Coram interjected. "Arthur Sutter has a bad heart and I keep telling him that brooding about the matter won't do his condition any good."

"Father, Mr. Sutter can't forget about those

jewels," said Penelope. "And even more important than that, he can't forget about the baby Christopher. What if he is still alive?"

"Pen, if he had somehow survived the earthquake, he would certainly have shown up long before now."

"Not if he didn't know who he was," Esther Greenway interposed. "I have always wondered if Christopher was kidnapped."

"The Sutters would certainly have known if their own child was kidnapped!" Dr. Coram replied with feeling.

"You forget, Dudley, that the father, Quentin, was killed and the mother was already dead by the time the earthquake happened," Esther Greenway reminded him. "The Sutters were the wealthiest people in the entire state back then. Even without the jewels they were certainly a target for kidnappers."

"It's just a lot of talk," Dr. Coram said, rising from his chair.

"I think it's a fascinating story," Penelope challenged.

"That's all it is, a story, Pen," replied her father, patting her on the shoulder. "The trouble with you is you don't have enough friends. You just sit in this big house thinking about all this and building it up into something that never happened."

"If Marge and Miss Sand would stay here for the rest of their vacation maybe I wouldn't get so lonesome!" Penelope answered, laughing.

"Won't you two stay? You would be doing me a real favor!"

"Oh, Penelope, that would be grand!" Marge cried. "But Susan and I have planned to return to Thornewood by Tuesday. My mother and I own a bookstore near Irongate University and I must get back to help her."

"You can't work with a bad sprain like that, can she Father?" Penelope insisted.

"Well, Marge, you might be able to hobble around the store on crutches," replied the doctor. "But I wouldn't advise putting any weight on that ankle until the swelling goes down. You could do permanent damage."

"Marge, I think you should take advantage of Penelope's generous offer," Susan stated. "Your mother has often taken care of the bookstore by herself. Now that the term at the university is underway, business isn't so heavy."

"I want you to stay, too, Miss Sand," Penelope urged, taking Susan's hand. "You can do your research for your book just as easily here as in Foxboro. And you will be making me very happy."

"Very well!" Susan answered, pressing the girl's hand warmly. "I can't refuse such an enthusiastic hostess. But my cat, Ikhnaton, Icky for short, is going to miss me."

"Miss Greenway and I love cats!" Penelope exclaimed. "You must bring him here. Oh, what fun we will have! Maybe, Miss Sand, *you* will be able to solve the mystery of the Sutter jewels and the disappearance of the baby Christopher.''

''I admit that I am intrigued,'' Susan Sand replied. ''I have never attempted to solve an eighty-year-old mystery!''

''You might as well give up that idea before you begin, young lady,'' Dr. Coram warned. ''You will just be wasting your time.''

''Perhaps you are right, Doctor,'' Susan Sand replied, but already her keen mind was at work.

Susan was the only one who knew about the face of the old woman at the window. Could there possibly be any connection between that wrinkled face and a mystery more than three quarters of a century old?

Chapter III

The Tower Room

"HOW THRILLING it is going to be to have you stay with us!" exclaimed Penelope. "Miss Sand, you must have the Tower Room! You'll have plenty of privacy for your writing and there is a wonderful view because it's up so high. Let me show it to you!"

"I'll take the Tower Room on one condition," Susan replied, rising from her chair. "You must call me Susan."

"Very well, Susan," answered Penelope, laughing. "I'm not used to having a famous author as a house guest!"

"You'll love the Tower Room if you don't mind climbing two flights of stairs," Esther Greenway offered. "And Marge, we will give you a room here on the first floor so you won't have any stairs to worry about."

"Our clothes are all in Foxboro at the inn," Marge replied. "We don't have as much as a toothbrush with us."

"For tonight, we can provide everything you will need," Dr. Coram interjected. "And I'll telephone the stables in Foxboro to let them know where their horses are."

"Tomorrow morning I'll go into town and pack up our things," Susan said. "My car is at the Foxboro Inn."

"It is very kind of you to want us as guests," Marge added, her freckled face flushing. "I can't thank you enough for all you have done."

"But you are doing us the favor by staying." Penelope replied. "And now, Susan, the Tower Room!"

As Susan Sand followed the excited girl out of the living room, her mind was a mixture of conflicting thoughts. Dudley House had an atmosphere that was difficult to define. The house was huge and furnished in the ornate style of Victorian times. There was something charming, yet oppressive, about the dark wood, heavy drapes, thick rugs, and high ceilings. Both Penelope and Esther Greenway were cheerful, pleasant people, and Dr. Coram was gracious and hospitable; but he was also opinionated and overbearing and made Susan feel uncomfortable.

"What would they all think if I were to tell them about the face of the old woman in the window!" Susan thought. "Would they know who she is? Perhaps she is a local character and there is nothing sinister in the incident."

"See how high up we are, Susan," exclaimed Penelope, throwing open a door at the top of a steep flight of stairs and switching on the light. "This is the Tower Room."

Susan stepped into a large, square room with a high ceiling and big, round windows in each wall. The furnishings were lavish. An enormous, elaborately carved bed stood in one corner, a heavy oak bureau in another, and an easy chair covered in red velvet against the wall facing them. Just inside the door was a desk and chair.

"It's lovely," said Susan, walking over to one of the windows. "Oh, there's a balcony! Is one able to go outside?"

"Of course," Penelope replied, opening the other door. "You can walk all around the tower, but be careful. The railing is very old and some people have a tendency to get dizzy when they look down."

Cautiously, Susan stepped out onto the balcony. The panorama was truly breathtaking. The Tower Room rose above the rest of the house like an immense chimney. In the moonlight Susan could see Raggedrock Ridge looming to her left and a stretch of woods spread out to her right. The sight was eerie, for the ridge looked like a set of jagged teeth, and the few twisted trees near the house seemed forlorn and grotesque.

Quickly, Susan walked around the entire balcony, then stood looking over to the stretch of woods.

"Those woods seem very thick," she said to Penelope, who had remained standing in the doorway.

"They belong to the Sutter property," the girl replied. "Arthur Sutter is immensely rich and owns acres and acres of land. His mansion is beyond the woods. We must visit him. He lives alone and loves having company. He likes to talk about the Sutter jewels and baby Christopher's disappearance, even though Father thinks it is bad for his heart."

"I would like to meet him," Susan replied. "But I wouldn't want to upset him."

"Personally, I don't think that talking about the earthquake upsets him nearly as much as Father seems to think," Penelope stated. "Father is always so concerned about his patients."

"Who else lives here in Dudley House besides you and your father and Miss Greenway?" Susan asked, trying not to sound intrusive.

"It's just the three of us," Penelope replied. "We have a groom for the horses, George Reger, but he lives in Foxboro. The house is much too big for three people. That's why we are so happy to have visitors."

Soon Susan was settled in the Tower Room of Dudley House. Esther Greenway had brought up everything that would be needed until morning. On the first floor, Marge was given a large, airy room that looked out on Raggedrock Ridge. Dr. Coram had provided her with a pair of crutches, and when Susan came down the two flights to see how her red-haired friend was faring, she found her hobbling around the room, laughing.

"I'll probably fall and break my arm!" Marge

cried out as Susan entered the room. "Dr. Coram doesn't know how long I will need these. Oh, Sue, aren't we lucky to have found such nice people when we needed them. And Dr. Coram is just wonderful!"

"He certainly is a good doctor," Susan replied, dropping onto Marge's bed.

"I don't think you like him, Sue," Marge returned, her face sobering.

"Sssh, Marge," cautioned her raven-haired friend. "He might hear you. Listen, I have something strange to tell you."

Briefly, Susan told Marge about the face of the old woman staring in at them while they drank their after-dinner coffee.

"A face! Of an old woman! Staring in through the window! How odd!" Marge said, her voice low. "Susan Sand, no wonder you jumped at the invitation to stay here! I thought there was something ulterior in your manner. You've discovered another mystery!"

"Just think, Marge," Susan continued, her green eyes shining. "There's a mystery about the Sutter jewels and possibly an old kidnapping, and besides that, there is that wrinkled face at the window! How could I miss such an opportunity?"

"But who could she be?" Marge asked, her brow wrinkling. "And why would she creep up to a house in the dark and stare in the window? Why, we're out in the middle of nowhere!"

"She was extremely interested in Penelope,"

Susan went on. "I simply must find out who she is. I got the definite feeling that she wanted to communicate with me."

"I would think she would be sorry that you saw her," Marge reasoned. "If she is up to no good, she must want to keep her presence a secret."

"I felt that she was sad, even frightened, but then perhaps my imagination is working over-time. After all, I saw her for only a few seconds. But I must find her and talk to her."

"Sue, I don't know how you manage to get in-volved in something scary no matter where we go," Marge chided, gingerly settling down in an easy chair and putting her injured ankle up on a footstool. "Sometimes I wonder why I don't avoid you like the plague!"

Suddenly a bulky figure loomed in the open door and both girls looked up, startled. The house was very quiet but neither Susan nor Marge had heard a sound. Dr. Coram stood looking in at the friends, stroking his moustache. He was smiling but there was something wary in his piercing blue eyes.

"I hope you two will be comfortable for the night until you can get your own things from Foxboro," he said, his voice low and his manner charming. "It's good for Penelope to have girls near her own age. She does get lonesome."

"We can't thank you enough for your hospital-ity," Susan replied, taking off her glasses and lev-eling her eyes on the doctor.

Dr. Coram bowed slightly and, without a word, turned and walked back down the hall.

"Sue, do you think he could have been listening?" Marge whispered, leaning forward in her chair. "I didn't even hear any footsteps. All at once he was just standing there."

"I don't think he could have been there long or we would have sensed his presence," Susan stated. "He's a strange man, Marge."

"He's mysterious," Marge replied. "The whole house is mysterious! Susan Sand, what have we gotten into?"

Chapter IV

Suspicion

IT was past midnight when Susan Sand climbed the steep stairs to the Tower Room. Outside a strong wind was blowing; the old house creaked and groaned. Electric lights had replaced the candle holders along the wall, but the staircase was still dim and shadowy. Susan opened the door and flicked the switch. The chamber, now flooded with light, seemed a safe haven from the rest of Dudley House.

Sitting on the huge bed, Susan contemplated her position. In just a few hours she and Marge had been thrust into a new mystery.

"Yet what do I know?" Susan asked herself, stretching out and putting her hands behind her head. "An old house, a strange doctor, and the face of an old woman looking in the window. Nothing but suspicion!"

For ten minutes Susan Sand turned the matter over in her mind.

"I need some facts!" she mused. "How can I

find that old woman? What could she tell me? Perhaps in the morning some brilliant idea will occur to me!"

Undressing, Susan slipped into a housecoat loaned to her by Miss Greenway and descended the stairs to the bathroom on the second floor. Once in the tub, Susan relaxed and soon found herself falling asleep! She was roused by the sound of voices coming from somewhere in Dudley House.

"Who could be talking at this hour?" she asked herself, climbing from the tub.

Quickly Susan dried herself, pulled on the nightgown loaned to her, wrapped the robe tightly, and crept from the bathroom. The voices drifted up to her from downstairs.

"That sounds like the back of the house to me," Susan thought, carefully descending to the first floor. "Dr. Coram's consulting room is at the end of the passage."

Susan tiptoed silently down the long hallway that led to the door of the doctor's private offices. A woman's voice, low but clear, seemed to be arguing with someone.

"I tell you, Dudley, that girl is a menace!" the woman said. "It is beyond me how you could ever agree to let her live here, even for a few days."

"Julia, will you please calm down!" a man answered, obviously Dr. Coram. "What else could I do? Turn the girls away? That would only have made them suspicious!"

"But Susan Sand! Dudley, she's dangerous. You know that as well as I. Look at that business of Witchwhistle Well this past summer. What if she were to find out anything!"

"That isn't going to happen," he replied, sounding very angry. "The other girl's ankle will be better soon, certainly within a week, and Susan Sand will be out of our lives."

Suddenly the door handle clicked. They were coming out! In a flash Susan flew back down the hall, opened the first door she came to, and found herself on a flight of stairs that apparently led to the basement.

"Oh, I hope they didn't see me!" she thought, carefully closing the door and grasping the wooden banister.

With her ear against the panel, Susan listened as footsteps came slowly toward the front of the house. Dr. Coram and "Julia" were still talking but their voices were barely audible.

" 'Julia' must be Julia Leck, Dr. Coram's office nurse," Susan told herself. "Penelope mentioned the name when we first arrived. If only I could get a look at her!"

At that moment Dr. Coram's voice could be heard very clearly just outside the cellar door. Then there was a grating sound.

"I lock the basement every night but your unannounced visit made me forget," said Dr. Coram, turning the key.

"He's locked me in the cellar!" Susan thought in panic as the voice of the doctor faded away.

"What a pickle!" Susan berated herself. "I'm a fine sleuth! And I don't even have my glasses on!"

Quickly Susan Sand found the light switch and stood looking down into a large, cluttered basement. An accumulation of years was piled in every corner, and she saw a big rat scurry toward its hole.

"There must be a window," she thought furiously. "If I can get outside maybe I can get back inside!"

Swiftly Susan made a tour of the basement. There were several windows which would serve as an exit but they were quite high up and very probably locked. Finding an old chair, Susan placed it under the most accessible one and climbed onto the sill. The window was either fastened or stuck. For five minutes the girl struggled but in vain. The next three windows proved to be just as tightly closed.

"That last one is my only hope!" she thought, pulling the chair beneath a small, dirty pane of glass.

"At least this one isn't locked, but it is definitely stuck!"

Susan pushed, pulled, and hammered, but still the window remained firmly closed.

"If I make any more noise I will certainly be heard," said Susan to herself. "I must have a tool."

Descending to the floor, Susan searched the

cellar for some kind of a lever. Soon she had found a large, sturdy chisel.

"This will do. Now for some wood-splitting!"

Susan Sand was not hefty but she was very strong and agile, and she soon had the little window open enough to squeeze through. However, a final thought occurred to her.

"I mustn't leave the light on or someone might become suspicious," she reasoned. "I'll just have to make my exit in the dark."

Susan lowered herself to the floor, climbed the stairs and switched off the light. Carefully she made her way back in the dark to the chair and up to the window. In a few moments she was free, covered with grime and cobwebs.

"Now I'm locked out! What a mess!"

The night was chilly, for the wind swept down from Raggedrock Ridge and swirled around the house. Susan Sand stood in the spindly shrubs that lined the foundation and looked about. If anyone were to come along, she would certainly be seen, for there was no cover whatsoever. The few trees near the house were too far away and too far apart to offer any protection.

Suddenly Susan heard voices.

"Julia Leck and Dr. Coram! She must be leaving!"

Two figures were standing talking next to a small car that stood in front of Dudley House.

"I can't go back into the basement! I must find

another window and climb into the house that way!''

Susan flattened herself against the shingles and edged carefully around the corner out of sight of the pair.

"I know!" Susan joyfully told herself. "Marge's room is on the first floor! She always sleeps with a window open!"

Hopefully, Susan tried to locate Marge's room. The floorplan of Dudley House was not yet clear in her mind, but she was quite certain that her friend's chamber was along this side of the structure.

"That should be it! Maybe I'll be in luck!"

Susan had spotted an open window near the farther corner. Hurrying over to it, she pulled herself up and looked in. The night was clear and there was a moon. Susan was able to see a sleeping figure across the room. Against the wall stood a pair of crutches.

"This is it!" she exulted, pushing the sash up further and drawing herself in. As she did so there was a clatter. Something had been knocked over! The figure in the bed stirred, then sat up. In another moment Marge was wide-awake. Before Susan had a chance to identify herself, the terrified redhead started to scream!

Chapter V

Arthur Sutter

MARGE SCREAMED again and again. Susan rushed over to the bed, but her friend lashed out wildly with her arms.

"Stay away from me!" she shrieked. "Help! Help!"

"Marge, be quiet! It's me. Susan! You'll wake the whole house!"

"Susan! Susan Sand!" said Marge, calming down somewhat.

"Yes. It's Susan. I got locked outside and had to climb in through your window."

"Susan Sand! You nearly gave me a heart tack. Climbing in my window! What time is it?"

"About two a.m. Listen, Marge. I hear footsteps. I must hide in the closet. Tell them you had a nightmare. I can't be seen."

Already doors were opening somewhere upstairs and Dr. Coram's voice could be heard outside.

Quickly Marge Halloran gathered her scattered wits.

"I don't know what you've been up to, Sue, but I'll put on a good act."

There was a loud knocking on Marge's door just as Susan slipped into the closet.

"What's wrong, young lady?" asked Dr. Coram.

"It's nothing, Doctor," replied the redhead. "I had a nightmare."

The door opened and Dr. Coram strode into the room. Behind him were Miss Greenway and Penelope.

"Marge, whatever is the matter?" asked Penelope, pushing past her father. "You look like a ghost!"

Marge smiled sheepishly and pulled the covers around her.

"I'm all right, Penelope. I'm subject to these dreams. Sometimes when I stay in a strange house they get very bad."

Dr. Coram came over to the bed and took Marge's wrist.

"Your pulse is racing like a trip-hammer," he said with a professional air. "I'll give you a sedative."

"Oh, no!" Marge protested. "I don't need anything. Once I adjust to my new surroundings I'll be fine."

Dr. Coram stood studying Marge, stroking his moustache.

"The entire day has been very exciting for

you,'' he replied. ''Does your ankle bother you?''

''Very little,'' Marge answered truthfully. ''I'm sorry to cause all this trouble. Please go back to bed.''

''Perhaps a nice glass of warm milk would help,'' suggested Miss Greenway.

''No. Nothing, thank you,'' Marge insisted, feeling more foolish every minute.

''I really think a sedative is in order, but if you don't want it, we'll leave you to get back to sleep,'' Dr. Coram replied. The trio left and Susan emerged from the closet.

''Now, Susan Sand, will you please tell me what this is all about!'' Marge whispered, her face flushed and her red hair in disarray. ''You're covered with dirt!''

Briefly Susan explained the conversation she overheard and her escape through the basement.

''So you see, Marge, your window was my only way of getting back into the house without being seen by Dr. Coram and Miss Leck.''

''Why should they be afraid of you?''

''They must be trying to cover up something,'' Susan answered, sitting on her friend's bed. ''I'm glad that this happened or I never would have known. Now I must find out the truth!''

Marge looked doubtfully at Susan Sand and slid down under the covers.

''Every time I associate with you, something happens,'' she stated. ''I like Penelope, and if her father and that nurse are involved in something criminal it would be very sad for her.''

"It's because of Penelope that we must find out the truth," Susan insisted.

"But how are you going to do that?"

"I must try to find that old woman. She knows something, or she wouldn't be looking in the window at Penelope."

"How can you find her? You don't know who she is or where she lives."

"This is a country place. Everyone knows everyone else. Certainly an old woman like that would be a local fixture."

"She might not be from around here," Marge reminded her.

"In that case, she will be more difficult to locate, but I must try!"

"Right now I feel like getting some more sleep! How are you going to get back to the Tower Room?"

Susan crept over to the door and quietly opened it.

"I think everyone is in their rooms," she said. "If I'm seen, I can say that I heard you scream, too."

"Good luck!" said Marge as Susan slipped into the hall.

Susan managed to reach her room without meeting anyone. Fearful of arousing suspicion by taking another bath, she wiped the dirt and cobwebs from her face, hands, and arms with her washcloth. Then she threw herself into bed and slept soundly until nine o'clock the next morning.

When Susan entered the breakfast room Marge, Penelope, and Miss Greenway greeted her.

"You missed all the excitement last night," said Marge. "I had another one of my nightmares."

"Oh, Marge, I'm sorry to hear that," replied Susan.

"I woke the entire house," Marge continued.

"I guess I didn't hear you because my room is so high up," Susan replied. "How are you feeling this morning?"

"Oh, I'm fine now," Marge answered. "My ankle feels much better."

"I'm so glad that you are going to stay with us," said Penelope. "Once you get used to your room, I'm certain your dreams will stop. Father says that it isn't uncommon in strange surroundings."

"Where is the doctor?" asked Susan.

"He's gone out on a house call," said Penelope. "And in this area that often means driving many miles."

"I'm very grateful to him," said Marge, glancing at Susan. "My ankle really is better."

"Just as long as you don't try to do too much," warned Penelope.

"And there are no more earth tremors!" replied Marge.

"I'll return the horses to the stables in Foxboro," said Susan. "And get our things from the inn. We didn't expect to be vacationing in Dudley House."

"The stable man, George Reger, said he would be glad to ride into town with you," Esther Greenway offered. "I think he is happy to have guests, too. He said he was anxious to meet the famous Susan Sand!"

After breakfast Marge telephoned her mother in Thornewood and Susan her Aunt Adele. Susan's aunt, a professor of art history at Irongate University, said she would be glad to drive out to Dudley House that afternoon and bring Icky, Susan's cat.

"My mother is relieved that I didn't break my leg!" laughed Marge. "I promised her no more horseback riding for a while!"

The groom, George Reger, proved to be an amiable man in his thirties who was glad of an opportunity to chat with Susan as they rode the horses into Foxboro.

"Do you like working for Dr. Coram?" Susan queried.

"I've been with him ten years and I like the job," he answered. "The doctor pays well but don't cross him! He has a nasty temper. But he cools down just as fast as he heats up!"

"My friend and I were very lucky to find him yesterday," replied Susan. "I was afraid that her ankle was broken."

"Funny thing, that earth tremor. I can't ever remember one before. Folks around here still talk about the terrible quake at the end of the last century. We should be thankful that it was just a tremor yesterday!"

"Dr. Coram thinks that the story about the Sutter jewels and the kidnapping of Christopher Sutter are just a legend," Susan continued.

"Oh, those jewels really disappeared," the man replied. "It's just a matter of *how* they disappeared! And there were quite a few people who were never found, so the baby could easily have been killed in the quake. I don't know why folks keep on talking about something that happened so long ago."

"Dr. Coram says that Arthur Sutter still talks a great deal about the story and that it upsets him," Susan went on. "Do you know Mr. Sutter?"

"Everyone around here knows Arthur Sutter," George Reger answered. "He's got a lot of money and he's generous with it, but he's not a happy man. Seems to me there is something bothering him."

"I understand that he has a heart condition," Susan stated.

"Yeah. He doesn't do much but he doesn't look sick. Just unhappy."

"Tell me, Mr. Reger, are there many old people in this area outside of the town of Foxboro?"

"Old people?"

"Yes. I would think that perhaps people would retire to a place like this."

"Well, there's old Mr. Hobbs. He owns a little farm quite a few miles from here. Aside from him, it's just the Corams and the Sutters."

"Does Mr. Hobbs have a wife?"

"Nope. He lives by himself except for some farm help."

Susan decided that further questions would provoke suspicion, but she reasoned that if the old woman lived in the area, George Reger would certainly know about her.

The town of Foxboro consisted of a main street, tree-lined and cobblestoned. There was the inn, some shops, a post office, library, town hall, church, and a few very old, quaint houses. The village had an interesting historical background and was a tourist attraction because of the excellent horseback riding trails and several antique shops.

After returning the horses to the stables and paying the owner for their use, Susan and George Reger strolled over to the Foxboro Inn. Soon Susan had packed Marge's and her belongings and paid the bill. Just as the pair emerged from the main entrance, a large, shiny blue limousine drew up in front of the library.

"That's Arthur Sutter's car," the groom explained. "It's a beaut!"

"Hello, George!" the millionaire called, climbing slowly out of the car.

Arthur Sutter was a tall, angular man with thick gray hair and sloping shoulders. He walked carefully over to Susan and the groom and shook hands.

"Mr. Sutter, this is Susan Sand," George Reger said.

"Susan Sand, the mystery story writer," Arthur Sutter replied. "I haven't yet read any of your books, Miss Sand, but I intend to. I'm happy to meet you."

"I've already heard a great deal about you, Mr. Sutter," Susan said, taking the man's extended hand. "My friend and I have been staying at Dudley House since yesterday afternoon."

Briefly Susan told the millionaire about Marge's mishap and about the Corams' hospitality.

"You must bring your friend over to my house," the man replied. "I live alone and don't have many people to complain to! We're just lucky that we didn't have another earthquake like the one eighty years ago!"

"We have been talking about that," Susan said. "I would like to hear what you have to say about it."

"Come back to my house now, and I will talk your ear off," Mr. Sutter offered.

"That is very kind of you, Mr. Sutter." Susan replied. "I would like that. I can drive in my own car."

"Why don't you let George drive your car back to Dudley House and you can come with me in my limousine," Arthur Sutter said.

"That's fine with me if Miss Sand doesn't mind my driving her car," the groom responded.

"Not at all, Mr. Reger," Susan replied, handing him the keys. "I'm glad to have an opportunity to chat with Mr. Sutter."

After dropping off some books in the box outside the library, Arthur Sutter got in the backseat of the big car next to Susan.

"I would like to drive myself," he said as the chauffeur pulled away. "But my heart condition prevents me. Dr. Coram insists that I take it very easy, so all I can do is talk!"

Susan Sand liked Mr. Sutter very much and admired his spirit. He chatted amiably about many topics while the limousine rolled along through an area that became increasingly woodsy. Soon a large house came into view. It was set among many trees and was approached by a circular driveway. The house was truly a mansion.

"It seems rather foolish to live in such a big place by myself, doesn't it?" Arthur Sutter said, reading Susan's thoughts.

"It's a beautiful house, Mr. Sutter," the girl responded. "You are really in the middle of the woods!"

"Yes. I own all this territory and I do love the house. But I like to have visitors, and I like to talk about the earthquake! I bet everyone told you that I don't talk about much else!"

Susan smiled.

"But, Mr. Sutter, that is just what I want to hear about. Ever since Marge and I arrived yesterday my curiosity has been aroused by what I have been told. I am very anxious to know what you think. Tell me about the Sutter jewels."

"They were brought back from India in 1854 by one of my ancestors, Bradley Sutter," he began. "They were never set but remained in the little leather pouch in the safe in the library here in the house. Even though I have never seen them, there is a record of what they look like. Two of them were perfect and the rest nearly so. They were considered a Sutter heirloom, and through the years some members of the family wanted to have jewelry made from them, but there was something about those beautiful, natural gems that was breathtaking. There were several dozen of them, including two large rubies, three huge diamonds, and one black pearl.

While Susan listened, fascinated, to Mr. Sutter, her gaze wandered over to the thick woods that surrounded the Sutter Mansion. For a moment she thought that her eyes were playing tricks, for the figure of a very old woman, frail and bent, appeared among the trees. As the car passed the spot, a wrinkled face, the very same face that Susan had seen the evening before in the window at Dudley House, peered out at her. Involuntarily, Susan gasped.

"It's the very same old woman!" she told herself. "I'd recognize her anywhere!"

Chapter VI

An Interesting Visit

"OH, if only I could follow her!" Susan thought furiously. "Who is she and what is she doing here on Mr. Sutter's property?"

Glancing at Mr. Sutter, Susan realized that he was unaware of the figure in the woods. In another moment the old woman was gone, vanishing into the thick underbrush.

"I can't think of anything that would please me more than to see those jewels," Mr. Sutter was saying. "Just think, Miss Sand, a black pearl, one of the most perfect ever found. Have you ever seen a black pearl?"

"No, never, Mr. Sutter," Susan replied as the limousine drew up in front of the Sutter Mansion. "Have you done anything to try to locate the jewels?"

"Years ago I hired a detective, but the man wasn't able to uncover one solid fact. There was just nothing to go on."

Stepping out of the car, Susan looked about.

"Miss Greenway is right," she thought. "The property is not at all well cared for."

The surrounding woods had advanced almost to the house and the mansion itself appeared neglected. The front door was opened by an elegantly dressed butler, but he seemed out of place. Entering the foyer, Susan was struck by an atmosphere of gloom.

"Come into the library," Mr. Sutter said, taking Susan's arm and hurrying her across a marble-floored hall. "I spend most of my time in this room. The rest of the house is hardly used. I have often wondered why I stay on here but I am a Sutter and I feel some kind of family loyalty."

The library, on the other hand, was cheerful and comfortably furnished with leather chairs, a thick, Persian rug, and a large desk. The walls were lined with glass-fronted bookcases.

"I must have the finest collection of books in this area," Mr. Sutter said, taking Susan's jacket and offering her a chair near a cheerful fireplace. "Better than the Foxboro library. But then I don't think there are very many people who would be interested!"

"I'm very interested," Susan replied sincerely. "And I know someone else who would love to look at these books, Professor Randall Scott of Irongate University. He is a good friend of mine."

"I've heard of Professor Scott," Mr. Sutter answered. "Isn't he the chairman of the History Department?"

"That's right. The youngest ever appointed to the post."

Mr. Sutter smiled.

"I can see that you think a great deal of Professor Scott," he stated.

Susan adjusted her glasses and leaned back in her chair.

"He and I have had some adventures together," she replied demurely. "And I respect him highly."

"You must bring him to see me. I've already told you how much I love to have visitors, especially interesting ones!"

"I'll extend the invitation the next time I see him," Susan promised.

The door opened and the butler entered with a tray. As he went about setting out coffee cups and little cakes, Susan's thoughts returned to the old woman. She had decided against telling Mr. Sutter about her.

"Perhaps there is something in the way she looked in the window, something that made me feel sorry for her," Susan told herself. "I must find her and talk to her!"

"There is another piece of jewelry that I forgot to mention," Arthur Sutter said, sipping his coffee. "Most people don't even know about it. It's a little, diamond-studded ring that was always placed on a chain about the neck of the baby of the family. When the earthquake occurred, that ring was probably on Christopher."

Rising from his chair, Susan's host went over to

a small wall safe and started turning the dial. Opening the door, he reached in and pulled out a small, black case and flipped up the lid.

"This little ring belonged to my grandfather when he was a baby. It is exactly like the one that would have been worn by Christopher Sutter."

Susan rose from her chair and crossed over to the safe. "It's beautiful!" she exclaimed, picking up the ring from where it lay on black velvet. "Look at all the tiny diamonds!"

"There's an inscription inside with my grandfather's name and the date of his birth. Christopher Sutter's would have a similar inscription."

"It must be extremely valuable," Susan surmised.

"Yes. The ring is a most unusual piece, especially designed for the Sutter babies. The others have been lost."

"Mr. Sutter, what do you think about the disappearance of Christopher?" Susan asked earnestly.

Arthur Sutter closed the box and returned it to the safe. Then, crossing back to his desk, he settled in his chair and leaned forward on the blotter.

"I think he was kidnapped and the Sutter jewels were the ransom," he replied, looking soberly at Susan. "After all this time it is almost a forgotten subject. But I can never forget about it. If Christopher Sutter were still alive he would be over eighty by now."

"If he were alive, wouldn't he have appeared long before this?" Susan gently asked.

"Of course he would have!" Arthur Sutter said with more vehemence than Susan would have expected. "But not if he didn't know who he was! That is what has always bothered me about the entire matter. What if Christopher Sutter lived his entire life or is still living it thinking he is someone else?"

Susan remained silent as Mr. Sutter leaned back in the leather chair.

"Oh, Susan, it's all foolish speculation!" he sighed. "But I hate unsolved mysteries!"

"Then you and I have a great deal in common," Susan returned. "If it is at all possible, I would love to solve this one. Penelope Coram told me the whole story just last evening."

"Penelope is a wonderful girl," Arthur Sutter stated. "I have talked to her a great deal about this. I don't think that you girls should get involved in it. It's too late."

"Nonsense!" Susan said defiantly. "You've aroused my curiosity so much I feel that I have to solve it!"

Arthur Sutter smiled warmly and sat studying his guest.

"Perhaps I should not tell you this, Susan, but Penelope Coram is an adopted child."

"Adopted!"

"Yes. Fifteen years ago when she was about a year old."

"Dr. Coram certainly seems like her real father. How did it come about?"

"She was adopted from the Wayside Orphanage, a reputable establishment about ten miles from here on the other side of Foxboro. A Miss Bingham, who still runs the institution, was in charge back then also."

"Why would he want to adopt a child?" Susan queried.

"Dudley Coram is a good man," Mr. Sutter stated. "He felt sorry for her."

"Penelope seems to be a happy girl," Susan answered. "Does she know that Dr. Coram is not her true parent?"

"Oh, yes. She was told when she was old enough to understand. Her adoption is no secret. Everyone around here knows. She is accepted as a Coram and people no longer think of her as anyone else."

"Somehow I feel, Mr. Sutter, that there is more to this than you are revealing," Susan returned, taking off her glasses.

"You are an unusually perceptive girl, Susan," he replied. "Yes. There were some puzzling circumstances surrounding Penelope's adoption."

Before Mr. Sutter could continue with his narrative, the door opened and the butler entered.

"There is someone to see you, sir," he announced. "Miss Julia Leck."

"Julia! On a Sunday. Well, it's an unexpected but pleasant surprise. Show her in, Kenneth."

"Miss Leck comes to give me injections for my

heart condition," Mr. Sutter explained. "But a Sunday visit is unusual."

Julia Leck entered the room and Mr. Sutter rose from behind the desk. She was an attractive, well-dressed blonde with an assured air.

"Julia. How nice to see you," he said, coming forward and taking her hand. "This is Susan Sand. Susan, Miss Leck."

"You're Susan Sand, the mystery story writer," said Miss Leck, gripping Susan's hand. "I was just at Dudley House, and I was so disappointed when George Reger told me you were over here I had to come right over to meet you! Now don't be insulted, Arthur, but Susan Sand is really the person I wanted to see!"

Susan shook the woman's hand and smiled graciously.

"What an actress she is!" Susan thought. "I doubt that she would be so charming if she knew that I overheard her conversation with Dr. Coram last night!"

Chapter VII

Raggedrock Ridge

"I LOVE your books," Miss Leck continued. "Why, just last week I finished *The Bony Finger*. I stayed up nearly all night to find out what would happen. You are very clever, Miss Sand."

"Thank you for the compliment," Susan replied. "But sometimes mysteries in real life are more interesting than those in books."

"Susan and I were discussing the earthquake and the Sutter jewels," Mr. Sutter offered. "Susan is not only good at writing mysteries, but at solving them as well."

"What is your theory about the baby Christopher, Miss Leck?" Susan asked, studying the woman intently.

Julia Leck perched herself gracefully on the edge of Arthur Sutter's desk. "It doesn't much matter what I think, does it?" she asked, smiling at Susan. "After all, everyone has his own pet theory about what occurred, but no one is going to discover anything after all this time."

"That is just what I was telling Susan," Mr. Sutter interjected. "But she told me she wants to solve it!"

"Really!" exclaimed Miss Leck, turning a penetrating gaze on Susan. "Have you been up to Raggedrock Ridge yet?"

"No, my friend and I were on our way there yesterday when the earth tremor happened," Susan answered coolly.

"Then you must let me take you," Miss Leck offered. "I have my car right outside."

"Is it possible to drive a car on such rocky ground?" Susan returned.

"There is another road up to the ridge besides the bridle trail," Mr. Sutter explained. "I often use it when I feel like seeing the view. It leads through my property and approaches the summit from the opposite direction of the riding trail."

"It is very kind of you to offer to take me there," Susan said to Miss Leck. "But do you really think that there is any chance of finding a clue after all these years?"

"That is the very question I should be asking you, Miss Sand," she returned. "You're the detective, aren't you?"

"What is she up to?" Susan asked herself. "She seems to be daring me to solve the mystery!"

"I have done some detective work in the past," the raven-haired girl replied, leveling her green eyes on the nurse. "I think that I will accept your offer to drive up and see the ridge. Perhaps I will discover something."

"Good!" Miss Leck exclaimed. "Let's go before it gets any later. I wish you could come with us, Arthur, but my car is really too small for more than two people."

"You and Susan go ahead," Mr. Sutter replied, ushering them to the door. "I feel rather tired. I think a short nap would be better medicine!"

"I've enjoyed our little talk, Mr. Sutter," Susan said, taking his hand.

"Promise you will visit me again and bring Professor Scott," the millionaire answered. "I'm looking forward to meeting him."

"I promise," Susan replied, following Miss Leck to her car.

"Who is Professor Scott?" Julia Leck asked casually, starting the engine.

"A friend of mine from Irongate University," Susan rejoined. "He's a historian. Mr. Sutter wants to show him his library."

"How interesting!" Miss Leck said. "I would like to meet him, too!"

Susan nodded her head but said nothing. The car drew away from the Sutter Mansion and headed through the woods.

"I understand that you work for Dr. Coram," Susan stated. "Have you known him a long time?"

"Oh, yes, many years," the nurse replied. "Dudley and I are both friends and colleagues."

"It was fortunate for my friend, Marge, that the doctor was so close by when the earth tremor happened," Susan said. "And it was very kind of him to offer to have us as houseguests."

"Dudley is a generous man," Miss Leck answered. "And I'm glad that Penelope can have some friends her own age in the house with her."

Susan Sand studied the nurse out of the corner of her eye as the car made its way up the winding, bumpy road that led to the summit of Raggedrock Ridge. The day had darkened somewhat and there was a hint of rain. Julia Leck guided the small car skillfully and chatted amiably about the area and the Sutter and Coram families.

"She is putting on an act and doing it very well," Susan thought. "If I hadn't overheard her conversation with Dr. Coram last night, I would think that she was truly delighted to have me stay at Dudley House!"

Raggedrock Ridge was a dismal-looking spot with huge boulders strewn about and a few tall, skinny pine trees. Stepping out of the car, Susan was buffeted by a sharp, cold wind that blew dirt in her eyes and whipped her raven hair about her head.

"The view from up here is lovely," said Miss Leck, noticing Susan's expression. "Over there is where Quentin Sutter is supposed to have met his fate."

Julia Leck pointed toward two enormous rocks that seemed to be stuck together. Along the top were jagged edges like the spine of some enormous sea monster. Susan followed the nurse as she made her way over the rocky ground.

"Apparently when Quentin Sutter reached this spot, the earth opened and his cloak got caught between these two boulders," Miss Leck explained. "In order to escape, he tore the cloak and tried to ride off on his horse, but the earthquake was so devastating and sudden he was thrown and killed. That is what people think."

"How dreadful," Susan murmured. "Are my eyes deceiving me, or is that really a piece of cloth stuck between those boulders?"

"That is the edge of the cloak," Miss Leck replied, "Even after all these years, some of the material remains."

Suddenly a figure appeared from behind the rocks. Susan jumped, startled. "Dr. Coram!" she exclaimed. "I didn't expect to see anyone!"

"What are you doing here, Dudley?" Miss Leck asked. "You frightened us!"

Dr. Coram smiled genially and made his way over to the pair. "Greetings, Julia, Miss Sand. I was on my way back from a house call and decided to stop," he explained. "I think that tremor yesterday did some damage. We are lucky that it was no worse!"

"I was showing Miss Sand the famous boulders," Miss Leck said. "But it's so chilly I think we should be getting back."

"I'll escort you to your car," the doctor replied. "Mine is over there." He pointed to a black sedan parked almost out of sight behind another group of rocks. "Let's go in this direction, out of the wind."

A light rain had started to fall as Susan and Miss Leck followed Dr. Coram.

"These shoes are bad for walking on this rocky ground," said the nurse, making her way carefully.

"It's a dangerous spot if you don't know the area," the doctor replied.

All at once Julia Leck slipped and fell against Susan, pushing her violently. Before the girl could get her footing, she slid into a small hole. The ground seemed to shift as the rocks moved under Susan's weight. Suddenly, the hole widened and she felt herself falling. Her hands grasped the air but there was nothing to hang on to. Susan Sand disappeared into the earth.

Chapter VIII

Accident?

"MISS SAND! Oh, my goodness!" cried Julia Leck."Dudley, she's fallen into a hole! We must get her out!"

"I told her this was a dangerous spot," the doctor replied, turning back. "These rocks are treacherous."

"Miss Sand! Miss Sand! Are you all right?" Miss Leck called, falling onto her knees and looking down into the gaping earth.

"I think I'm all right," called a voice. "At least I don't think that anything is broken."

"Don't move suddenly," Dr. Coram advised. "Flex each limb gently and make certain that there are no fractures."

Susan Sand followed the doctor's orders and managed to get slowly to her feet. . She was bruised and covered with dirt but nothing serious seemed to have occurred. Susan looked about. She was standing in a little cave about eight feet deep and three feet wide. Rocks were strewn around her where they had fallen when the ground gave way, but the area on which she stood was firm.

"That tremor yesterday obviously loosened the earth," Dr. Coram said, reaching his arm down into the hole. "See if you can grasp my hand. Perhaps I can pull you out."

Susan grabbed the doctor's hand with both of hers and with the help of Julia Leck, she was pulled to the edge of the crevice.

"Are you all right?" said Miss Leck solicitously, placing an arm around Susan's shoulder. "You could have been killed!"

"I'm fine," replied Susan. "Just dirty and a little bruised."

"Let me have a look at you," Dr. Coram interjected. "No. Nothing seems to be broken. You are a very fortunate young lady."

"My car is just over here," Miss Leck stated. "We'll help you into it and I'll drive you back to Dudley House."

Dr. Coram and Julia Leck carefully and gently escorted Susan to the nurse's car and helped her into the front seat. Miss Leck seemed genuinely concerned and Dr. Coram had assumed his most charming professional manner. Secretly, Susan Sand smiled to herself.

"I'll bet they wish I had fallen through to China!" she thought. "And they have to pretend how upset they are!"

"There," said Miss Leck, spreading a car robe

over Susan's knees. "Now, you just relax and we'll be back at Dudley House in a short time."

Dr. Coram returned to his sedan and the two cars moved off down the narrow road. Soon they were driving through the woods. During the trip Susan's mind raced.

"I wonder if that wasn't a planned accident?" she asked herself. "When Miss Leck slipped she seemed to push me on purpose. But I have no way of being certain!"

In about ten minutes the winding drive that led to Dudley House came into view.

"Look! There are two cars," cried Julia Leck.

"That's my aunt's car and Professor Scott's," said Susan. "Oh, I'm so glad they've arrived. I've missed Icky."

"Icky? Who is Icky?" Miss Leck asked, helping Susan from the car.

"My cat. Ikhnaton, Amenhotep IV," Susan replied. "Icky for short."

"A cat? You have a cat?" Julia Leck uttered. "And your aunt has brought him here?"

"Yes. He loves new places to explore, and Penelope said that she loves cats."

Once inside Dudley House Susan was greeted with hugs and kisses by her aunt, Adele Sand, a tall, distinguished-looking woman with gray hair and alert gray eyes. Susan's resemblance to her was unmistakable. Randall Scott, a husky, handsome young man with wavy brown hair and humorous brown eyes, stood by smiling. In his arms was a large, fluffy orange cat, its tail flicking nervously.

"What's happened to you, Susan?" Randall Scott asked. "There's dirt on your clothes and your arm is bruised."

Before Susan could answer, Dr. Coram introduced himself and Julia Leck and explained what had occurred on Raggedrock Ridge.

"Susan! You could have been seriously injured!" Professor Scott exclaimed, setting Icky on the rug.

"Goodness, Susan!" said her aunt. "I never know what is going to happen to you next!"

"I'm all right," Susan replied, looking fondly at Professor Scott. "I'm glad to see you all. And how are you, Icky?"

Susan swept up the big animal and gave him a kiss. Immediately he began to purr loudly.

"He sounds like an outboard motor," said Penelope, stroking Icky's silky head. "Susan, sit down and relax. You've had a frightening experience."

"How fortunate you didn't break your ankle!" added Marge.

Susan laughed and settled herself on the couch. Icky jumped to the floor and headed straight for Miss Leck.

"Look how he likes you, Julia!" Miss Greenway stated.

Icky had leapt onto the nurse's lap and was pawing vigorously at the belt on her dress. Miss Leck seemed unduly disturbed.

"Why does he like me?" she asked, trying to push the cat away.

"You have a cat, don't you?" Penelope noted. "Isn't his name Fussy? Icky and Fussy! They sound like a vaudeville team!"

"He can smell Fussy's fur on your dress," Susan reasoned. "I wonder if they would like each other?"

Miss Leck jumped up from her chair, and Icky sprang to the floor.

"You must come to tea, Miss Sand," she said rather abruptly. "I'm glad that nothing serious happened to you. Now, I really must be going. Promise you will come and see me. We still have a great deal to talk about."

"I would love to visit you and meet Fussy," Susan replied.

"Must you go so soon?" Dr. Coram asked.

"Yes, Dudley. I have things to do. It was nice meeting you, Professor Sand and Professor Scott." The nurse hurried to the door and rushed down the drive to her car.

"What got into her?" Penelope asked. "I never saw her act like that."

"Icky must have upset her, the way he was pawing at her dress," replied Marge.

"But Miss Leck loves cats. She treats Fussy as if he were a baby!" answered Penelope.

"I know Julia very well," Dr. Coram interrupted. "The excitement on Raggedrock Ridge has made her nervous."

Susan Sand adjusted her glasses and studied the

doctor. He was smiling in his genial way, but his eyes were wary.

"How odd!" the raven-haired girl thought. "What are they involved in? And what could Miss Leck's extraordinary reaction to Icky have to do with it?"

"I'm grateful that nothing serious happened to you, Sue," Randall Scott said, sitting on the arm of the couch and taking Susan's hand. "It seems that every time you are away from me, for even a short while, something dangerous occurs!"

Susan Sand laughed and looked up at the young man.

"Susan falls into a hole and I have a sprained ankle!" cried Marge. "Sue, you lead a charmed life!"

"Let's go up to the Tower Room," suggested Penelope. "I would like to show the view to your Aunt Adele and Professor Scott."

"I'll stay down here with Marge and Dr. Coram," said Miss Greenway as their young hostess led the way to the staircase. Icky gracefully padded ahead of them, his plumelike tail waving excitedly.

"How does he know where we are going?" Penelope asked.

"He doesn't," laughed Susan. "But he loves to explore and he wants to see the rest of the house!"

The little group climbed the steep steps to the Tower Room. All the way up Icky made sudden darts into the shadows, batting at anything that moved and mewing softly.

"He's a character!" exclaimed Penelope. "There's nothing to catch, Icky!"

Susan almost revealed that she had seen a rat in the basement the night before but fortunately restrained herself before the words slipped out.

At the top of the stairs Penelope opened the door and the group stepped inside.

"This is a lovely room," Professor Sand stated.

"See the balcony," replied Penelope. "Come outside. Raggedrock Ridge is over in this direction."

Aunt Adele followed the young girl out onto the wooden balcony but Randall Scott took Susan's arm and held her back.

"Susan, are you really okay?" he asked. "Perhaps it's my imagination, but there seems to be something strange about this house. Why did that nurse rush out of here so suddenly?"

"Sssh," replied Susan. "I don't want to worry my aunt, but I have a great deal to tell you. Can you stay?"

"Stay! Of course I can stay! I'll move in if that's what you want!"

"That's not what I meant!" Susan scolded. "But we must talk. I know that Aunt Adele has to get back to Thornewood. She has a heavy work load this semester."

"Susan, what has been going on?"

"I have no way of proving it, but I think that

Dr. Coram and Miss Leck are involved in something shady and that my fall on the ridge was no accident. Randall, I need your help!''

Chapter IX

At the Foxboro Inn

"WHAT ARE YOU two whispering about?" asked Penelope, looking in the door from the balcony. "You act as if you are plotting something. Come out here, Professor Scott, and see the view."

"It's a beautiful sight, Randall," Adele Sand added. "The sun is just beginning to set."

"I'll be right out," the young man called. Then, turning to Susan, he lowered his voice and smiled engagingly. "Susan Sand, you never said you needed me before, but the words are music to my ears," he murmured. "How about coming to dinner with me tonight and we can discuss everything in private."

"I'd love to," Susan replied. "Let's go to the Foxboro Inn. We can find a secluded booth where no one will bother us."

At that moment Icky pranced into the room and then back to the balcony, meowing loudly and looking over his shoulder.

"He wants us to come outside," laughed Susan, crossing to the door. "Oh, it is a lovely sight. Look at that red glow."

"What is that over there?" asked Penelope, pointing in the direction of the Sutter woods.

"It looks like a wisp of smoke," said Professor Sand. "Does anyone live in those woods?"

"I don't think so," returned Penelope. "Perhaps Mr. Sutter's gardener is burning leaves."

"He wouldn't do it in the middle of the woods," replied Randall Scott.

"I wonder what could be causing it," mused Susan, adjusting her glasses. "Perhaps it is smoke from a chimney. Are there any houses in that direction?"

"The Sutters once had a lot of servants and some of them did live in little cottages on the property quite far from the mansion, but I doubt if anyone would be living there now. Who would it be?"

"I can't imagine," Susan replied. "I'll have to ask Mr. Sutter the next time I see him. He is very anxious to meet you, Randall."

"Arthur Sutter, the millionaire?" Professor Scott queried. "I've heard of him. I would like to meet him. He must know a great deal about this entire area."

"He has a tremendous library," Susan said. "He wants you to see it. Perhaps tomorrow I can call him."

Since the air was beginning to get chilly, the

little group returned inside and Professor Adele Sand prepared to depart.

"I would truly like to stay longer," she said as the party filed down the stairs. "But I have classes tomorrow and papers to correct."

"I'm so glad you could come and bring Icky," Penelope replied. "And we are delighted to have Susan and Marge stay. I just wish they would remain forever!"

"What are your plans, Randall?" Aunt Adele asked. "It would suit me if you stayed and prevented my niece from falling into any more holes!"

"Susan has consented to come to dinner with me in Foxboro," the young man replied, his brown eyes twinkling. "If there's room for me at the inn there, I would like to stay on awhile."

"I hope our having dinner out won't inconvenience you, Penelope," Susan said.

"Of course not," the girl replied. "Marge and Miss Greenway and Icky and Father and I can all dine together! Icky can have caviar if he wants it!"

Several hours later Susan Sand and Randall Scott were seated in a dim corner of the charming Colonial dining room of the Foxboro Inn.

"This is the perfect place to talk," said Susan, looking over the menu. "No one will disturb us."

"I hate to disillusion you, young lady," returned Randall Scott, "but that fellow over there who just came in seems to be very interested in you."

"Oh, that's George Reger, the groom at Dudley House," Susan explained as the young man approached their booth.

"Miss Sand, I don't want to butt in," he began as he reached the table. "But I heard about your accident on Raggedrock Ridge. Sure glad you're okay. It's a good thing that Dr. Coram and Miss Leck were with you or you might never have gotten out of that hole!"

"It's very kind of you to be so concerned," Susan replied. "Fortunately, nothing serious happened."

The groom bowed rather clumsily and moved off toward a table across the room. Nearby, an elderly, white-haired woman with a pleasant face and shrewd blue eyes nodded at him as he passed her chair.

"How d'do, Miss Bingham," said George Reger. "Good to see you again."

"Hello, George, nice to see you, too," she replied, continuing with her dinner.

Susan Sand turned her head at the name Miss Bingham.

"That must be the administrator of the Wayside Orphanage," Susan explained. "I distinctly remember that Mr. Sutter said her name was Bingham."

"The Wayside Orphanage?"

"Yes. Mr. Sutter told me that Penelope Coram

is adopted and that Miss Bingham was in charge at the time fifteen years ago.''

"Really?" Randall Scott murmured. "Rather odd, isn't it, for a bachelor to adopt a baby." Then in his authoritative voice he said, "But what I want to hear is everything that happened to you since yesterday afternoon. And I mean everything!''

Carefully Susan Sand went over the events of the previous day, trying not to omit anything of importance. Randall Scott seemed totally disinterested in his food as he listened to Susan's story. His fork lay on his plate and his wine sat untouched. When Susan finished talking, he sat back and sighed.

"Sue, I find it hard to believe that so much could have happened to you in twenty-four hours. What do you do? Look for trouble?''

"Perhaps it looks for me!" she retorted. "One of the most intriguing things is that old crone. Who is she and why would she be looking in the window at Penelope? And why was she flitting about on Mr. Sutter's property?''

"There are so many questions to be answered," the professor replied. "It's obvious Dr. Coram and Miss Leck, knowing your reputation, are worried about what you might discover. Why did she rush out of Dudley House this afternoon after Icky pawed at her dress?''

"Wasn't that strange!" Susan rejoined, her green eyes shining. "She loves cats and yet she couldn't get away from Icky fast enough!''

"My main concern is for your safety," Randall Scott said, reaching across the table and taking her hand. "That pair intended to harm you up there on the ridge."

"Perhaps they just wanted to scare me off," Susan replied.

"Whatever their intentions, I don't want to leave you here alone."

"Randall, I do want you to help me solve this. Perhaps you could get a room here at the inn."

"I know that I'm not going back to Thornewood. Not yet," he stated firmly. "Tonight I will stay here at the inn. We have to make plans!"

At that moment the waiter came over and handed Susan a note. Quickly she opened the small envelope and drew out a piece of paper.

"Dear Miss Sand," the note began. "Please do not think that I am imposing on you and your friend, but it is imperative that I speak to you tonight. Would it be possible for you to come to my apartment at the Wayside Orphanage? Take Route #43 West, turn left on Pine Lane for half a mile. If you can come, nod your head. I will leave before you. Lynn Bingham."

Susan read the message and passed it over to Randall Scott. His eyes widened as he read the words. Susan nodded and smiled at Miss Bingham who immediately rose and left the dining room.

"What could she want?" Susan whispered, finishing her dessert. "She insists that we see her tonight!"

"She looks like a shrewd old lady to me," he replied, rising from his chair and calling the waiter. "Let's get to the Wayside Orphanage as fast as possible!"

Chapter X

Miss Bingham's Story

"THERE'S A SIGN for Pine Lane," cried Susan, leaning out the window of Randall Scott's car. "Miss Bingham's note said that the Wayside Orphanage is about a half a mile."

"We are certainly in the country," replied the young man, turning off the highway. "This road is not very well lighted."

"She couldn't be very much ahead of us the way we hurried out of the inn," Susan said. "I think she was driving that green convertible that left the parking lot just before we did."

"Whatever she has to say must be extremely important, or she could have waited until tomorrow," Professor Scott reasoned.

"She used the word *imperative* in her note," Susan added.

Soon a sprawling structure that resembled a large farmhouse came into view. The building was set back from the road and surrounded by an iron fence.

"Since there is nothing else in sight this must be the orphanage," Susan said. "We've come at least half a mile."

"There's Miss Bingham herself motioning to us from the gate," exclaimed Professor Scott.

The small, white-haired woman was waving her arms, signaling them to drive in.

"I'm so glad you could come," she said as the car drew to a halt. "You must think that I am half-mad getting you out here at this hour, but I was afraid to let any time pass. I'm Lynn Bingham and I run the Wayside Orphanage."

"This is Professor Randall Scott, Miss Bingham," replied Susan. "We came as quickly as we could."

"You've made me feel better already, Miss Sand," the woman replied. "If you will just park over there, Professor, you can both come into my apartment where we can talk."

In a short time Susan Sand and Randall Scott were seated in Miss Bingham's cheerful living room sipping coffee and waiting for an explanation from their hostess.

"First, let me say that I heard you were in Foxboro, Miss Sand," began the administrator. "Since this is such a small place, gossip travels fast. I learned of your friend's mishap yesterday and of your staying at Dudley House. What prompted me to call you here was what I heard

George Reger say back there at the Foxboro Inn."

"You mean about my fall on Raggedrock Ridge," Susan answered. "I wasn't hurt."

"Thank heavens for that!" Miss Bingham returned. "How did the accident happen?"

"Miss Leck slipped and fell against me, pushing me onto some loose rocks which gave way," Susan explained.

"Oh, dear!" sighed Miss Bingham, leaning back in her chair. "I feared as much. It is imperative that I tell you my experience but it is difficult to know where to begin. I don't want you to think that I am a foolish old woman."

"Oh, we could never think that!" Susan and Randall Scott cried in unison.

"It is kind of you to take such an attitude," she replied, smiling warmly. "But wait until you have heard my story before you come to any conclusions. I really must begin fifteen years ago. At that time I was in charge of the orphanage as I am now, but I did a great deal more of the actual work with the children. Today my position is almost completely administrative, although I try to visit each child every day.

"I have always lived in this apartment right here on the grounds in order to be available to anyone who may need me. Fifteen years ago—I remember that it was also a Sunday evening—I was here in my apartment reading when I heard a baby crying very loudly. Of course, that is nothing unusual in an orphanage, but this sound was definitely coming from outside!

"The night was rather warm, for it was June, but I slipped on a sweater and hurried down to where I had heard the crying. As I arrived at the main entrance, the door opened and the night nurse came out. She, too, had heard the sounds. There on the doorstep, was a basket with a baby inside, wailing pitifully!"

"Had that ever happened before?" Susan asked, adjusting her glasses. "A baby being left on the doorstep?"

"No, never before in all my experience, Miss Sand," Miss Bingham replied. "Our children are usually received from hospitals and other institutions. This child was about a year old with light red hair and a beautiful face. The night nurse and I immediately brought her inside and I made out the proper forms, took the child's footprints and fingerprints, and placed her in one of our cribs in the nursery. Now the problem was to find out who she was and where she had come from. Since it was Sunday evening, there was nothing I could do until the next day, so I retired for the night and pondered the entire situation."

"Miss Bingham, that baby was Penelope Coram, wasn't it?" Susan asked, leaning forward eagerly.

"Yes, Miss Sand. The baby was Penelope. The next morning, Julia Leck arrived for work. At that time she worked several days a week here, as she still does, and the rest of the time for Dr. Coram. As soon as I saw her, I told her about the baby. She immediately went to the nursery to see the child. When she returned, I was about to go into the basement where we keep all our old records. As I opened the door and started down the stairs, Miss Leck hurried by and apparently without thinking, pushed the door closed. She shoved so hard that I went tumbling down the stairs and hit my head on the cement floor. Immediately I lost consciousness."

"Oh, how terrible!" exclaimed Susan.

"When I awoke I was in the hospital in Linton, twenty-five miles away! Fortunately, I had broken no bones, but I did have a mild concussion and was forced to spend several days in the hospital. On my return to the orphanage one of the first things I did was to go to see how the new baby was. To my amazement she was gone! She had been adopted by Dr. Coram!"

"Was that a usual procedure?" asked Randall Scott. "To have a baby adopted in so short a time?"

"No, Professor Scott," Miss Bingham replied. "It was most unusual. Since no one knew who this child was, my intention had been to notify the police and start an investigation. I certainly didn't want the child removed from the orphanage before I had done all I could to find out her identity. I confronted Dr. Coram on the subject and he assured me that he would launch his own investigation."

"Had the doctor ever shown any interest in adopting a child before?" Susan queried.

"Never to my knowledge," Miss Bingham replied vehemently.

"Did he ever conduct an investigation as he said he would?" Professor Scott asked.

"Oh, yes. He called in the police, and for a while there were headlines in all the newspapers about this beautiful baby that had been left on the doorstep of the Wayside Orphanage. The papers loved the story! But nothing was ever discovered about Penelope's identity."

Miss Bingham sat and studied her two guests for several moments.

"You must be puzzled as to why I called you out here to tell you a story which you would have heard sooner or later," she said, a worried expression in her blue eyes.

"No, Miss Bingham. I think that I understand," Susan Sand replied, meeting the woman's gaze. "You believe that I am in danger because of my fall on Raggedrock Ridge. All these years you have been suspicious about your tumble down the basement stairs."

"Yes, Miss Sand. I have always wondered if Miss Leck intentionally shoved that cellar door closed so that I would fall," Miss Bingham answered. "Did she want me out of the way so that Dr. Coram could adopt Penelope before someone else did?"

"Pushing you would be a criminal act!" cried Randall Scott.

"I couldn't go to the police," the administrator returned. "All I had to go on was suspicion. Then as time passed and Penelope seemed happy at Dudley House, I began to think that I had imagined the entire episode. But something happened yesterday morning to arouse my suspicions all over again, even before I learned of your fall, Miss Sand. Usually on Saturdays I drive over to see my sister. The trip is about thirty miles, and sometimes I spend the night. Yesterday, however, I changed my plans and stayed here at the orphanage.

"About ten o'clock in the morning I came into the main building to visit the children. Just as I reached my office I heard a noise behind me. The basement door opened and Julia Leck emerged. She didn't see me but hurried out the main entrance and drove off in her car."

"What could she have been doing?" Susan asked.

"I can come to only one conclusion," Miss Bingham replied. "We keep all the old records on every child that we have ever had here at the orphanage. They are all carefully filed alphabetically in metal file cabinets in the basement. As soon as Miss Leck was gone, I went down to the cellar and looked over the folders. The one on Penelope had been disturbed and replaced out of order. I am convinced that Julia Leck, knowing that I am usually away on Saturday, and wanting for some reason to see that folder, came to the orphanage for just that reason. In her haste, and afraid of being caught, she neglected to put the folder back properly."

"Why would she want to look at Penelope's baby records after all these years?" Susan asked.

"It's odd," Miss Bingham replied. "But, more importantly, why would she and Dr. Coram want to harm you?"

"This is far more serious than I ever would have imagined," said Susan Sand, breathing deeply. "Who is Penelope and why did Dr. Coram adopt her?"

Chapter XI

In the Woods

"WHO IS PENELOPE?" said Miss Bingham, repeating Susan's words. "Many times during the past fifteen years I have asked myself that question. I seldom see the Corams, but from what I have heard, the girl is happy."

"Has anything else ever happened to make you suspicious of Miss Leck?" Susan asked.

"No. Nothing. The woman has been charming to me," the administrator replied. "Except for that one incident where she closed the door on me so suddenly, I have never felt any fear of her."

"How does Dr. Coram treat you?" Professor Scott queried.

"Cordially," Miss Bingham replied. "He comes here to the orphanage to see some of the children several times a week. I sometimes wonder if my imagination didn't get the better of me."

"It isn't your imagination," Susan firmly stated. "They are an extremely clever pair."

"But why would Dr. Coram want to adopt a child when he never expressed any interest before?" Randall Scott said, almost to himself.

"We must discover Penelope's identity," Susan replied. "Miss Bingham, I have had a peculiar experience since I arrived at Dudley House yesterday."

Briefly Susan told her about the old crone looking in the window at Penelope and her fleeting appearance on Mr. Sutter's property.

"I have never seen such a person as you describe," Miss Bingham said. "She is certainly not from around here."

"Then who is she and why does she keep appearing?" Professor Scott asked.

"The entire mystery centers around Penelope," Susan stated. "Miss Bingham, we can't thank you enough for your help. You took a chance asking us to come to see you and telling us your story."

"It was an impulsive decision," Miss Bingham replied. "Now that I have heard your experience, I am glad that I decided to take you into my confidence."

"There is one other thing that you should know," Susan interjected. Quickly she told the woman about the conversation she had overheard between Miss Leck and Dr. Coram.

"Then they are up to something!" Miss Bingham cried. "Oh, Susan, you are in danger!"

"Please don't worry about me," the girl replied, placing her hand on the woman's arm.

"Randall is taking a room at the Foxboro Inn and between us we should be able to solve the mystery. If only we could find that old crone!"

"That's not going to be easy, especially since she is not from this area," Randall Scott warned her.

"The difficulty is that we don't want anyone else to know about her," mused Susan. "Not even Mr. Sutter. We must find her on our own."

"I wish you luck," Miss Bingham replied earnestly. "And please be careful!"

Susan and Randall thanked the administrator for her hospitality and promised to keep her informed about the progress of their investigation. On the way back to Dudley House, the professor came to a sudden decision.

"Let's go up to Raggedrock Ridge," he said. "I'm anxious to see the spot."

"It's a lovely moonlit night," Susan noted. "The view is truly a panorama. Do you know that it is after midnight?"

"A perfect time to go sightseeing!" Randall Scott decided.

"Perhaps I won't be able to find the way!" replied Susan, laughing. "There is a road that leads through Mr. Sutter's property. I hope I can find it!"

Because the night was so clear and bright, Susan Sand was able to guide her friend to the top of Raggedrock Ridge. When they arrived, she immediately took him over to the two huge boulders which gave the ridge its name.

"In the daylight, you can still see a piece of the cloak that Quentin Sutter was wearing when the earthquake happened," she explained.

"Extraordinary!" exclaimed Professor Scott. "What damage must have been done back then. It's a good thing that tremor yesterday was no worse."

"According to Dr. Coram, there was some damage," Susan replied.

"I hate to think of your being up here with that pair!" Randall Scott said, taking Susan's hand. "Sue, you could have been killed."

"Don't think about that," she returned. "Look at this beautiful view!"

"It is lovely," he agreed.

"Oh, look! Over there! Isn't that smoke?" Susan asked.

"Yes. It is smoke. It is very clear in this moonlight."

"Remember how this afternoon in the Tower Room Penelope pointed out smoke coming from just about the same spot?" Susan recalled. "What could be causing it?"

"A house, perhaps?"

"Penelope did say something about old servants' cottages. Oh, Randall, let's go and investigate!"

"I'm game! But we will have to walk after we reach the woods. I have a flashlight in my car, so we should be able to find our way."

Soon the pair was approaching the large expanse of woods that made up a great deal of the

Sutter land. The road that branched off from the main one dwindled to nothing but a dirt path, and Randall Scott was forced to park the car in a small clearing.

"It's on foot from here on!" he announced, flicking on the flashlight. "What direction do you suggest?"

"Straight ahead!" Susan answered. "We'll probably get lost!"

Carefully Susan Sand and Randall Scott made their way through the thick woods in the direction from which they had seen the smoke. Fortunately, Susan carried a compass in her bag so that their bearing was always clear.

"Those were the good old days, way back when servants had their own cottages," Randall Scott remarked.

"Yes. Apparently when the Sutters were a large family, they had a crew of servants. That was when servants were plentiful."

"Is it possible that someone is living in one of those cottages?"

"Mr. Sutter never mentioned it. Certainly it would be odd nowadays to have a servant in the middle of the woods so far from the mansion."

Diligently, the pair advanced, wondering with every step if they were not making a foolish mistake, for the woods covered a large area. Any hope of finding the cottage seemed remote when they faced the reality of their task.

"Without this flashlight, we couldn't see at

all," Randall Scott noted. "Fortunately the batteries are new."

"Randall, I think I smell smoke!" Susan announced triumphantly.

The pair stopped and sniffed the air.

"Yes. It is smoke!" he agreed. "We're in luck, for it's quite pungent. We must be close to its source."

Susan and Randall walked on for several hundred feet when a gap appeared in the trees.

"Look! A cottage!" Susan whispered.

"There is a dim light coming from inside," Randall Scott added.

A small structure, dilapidated and overgrown with foliage, stood in a natural clearing which was bordered by huge pine trees. A faint glow brightened the front windows.

"Oh, Randall! This is exciting! Someone is living there!"

Stealthily the pair crept up to one of the windows and peered in. Susan gripped Randall Scott's arm, for by the fireplace stood a figure, stirring the embers with a poker.

"It's the old crone!" Susan gasped close to his ear.

"Incredible!" Randall Scott replied. "She must be close to a hundred!"

"What does she have in her hand?" Susan asked.

The old woman had replaced the poker and was fingering something which gleamed in the light of the fire.

"It looks like a piece of jewelry," he remarked.

Susan Sand adjusted her glasses and studied the object dangling from the woman's hand.

"I think she is holding a gold chain," Susan said. "Look at the expression on her face. She's handling it as though it were a precious object!"

At that moment the crone turned her head and two bright, black eyes looked directly at the window. Instantly, Susan and Randall Scott drew back.

Chapter XII

A Discovery

SILENTLY Susan Sand and Randall Scott edged along the wall of the cottage away from the window and into the protection of the trees. Several seconds later the sash was raised and a lantern appeared. By its glow Susan and Randall could see the wrinkled face peering earnestly out into the darkness, holding the lantern first on one side and then on the other. Apparently satisfied that no one was there, the old woman closed the window, and the light disappeared.

"I'm so anxious to talk to her," Susan whispered. "But how will she react if we approach her at this hour and without any warning?"

"Did she see our faces?" he asked.

Suddenly the door opened and the bent figure emerged, wrapped in a dark cloak and carrying the lantern. She looked about and started in the direction where Susan and Randall were hiding but was obviously unaware of their presence, for she trudged off into the woods.

"Where could she be going?" Susan murmured. "Oh, Randall, let's follow her!"

The young professor nodded a silent assent and the pair started after the old crone, trying to keep far enough behind so as not to be heard. She seemed to be certain of her destination, for she walked at a rapid pace, and her pursuers found that they were almost jogging.

"She's in good condition even if she is ancient!" Randall Scott said, smiling. "I can think of several fellows on the Irongate football team who aren't in such shape!"

The trek continued for several miles, the woman never slackening her pace and always heading in the same direction, the lantern swinging in her hand. She seemed to be muttering to herself, for every so often a few words drifted back to Susan and Randall.

"I must find them," she said distinctly. "They have to be there."

"What is she talking about?" the young man said.

"Perhaps we'll find out," Susan replied. "Randall, she's heading for Raggedrock Ridge!"

The woods were beginning to thin and the jagged teeth of the mountain chain came into view. The moonlight now made undetected pursuit difficult, and the pair was forced to drop further back. The old crone barely slowed her pace as the ground began to rise and she continued to murmur to herself.

"She is certainly going to the top of the ridge," Randall Scott decided. "What is she up to?"

"I think that I am beginning to understand," Susan replied. "Randall, we must not be seen! Let's wait until she reaches the summit. Then we can climb up and watch her."

They stopped and watched the woman in her ascent. When she arrived near the two jagged rocks that gave the ridge its name, Susan pulled Randall Scott's arm and they started up after her. By the time they reached the top the old crone was nowhere in sight.

"Where did she go?" Susan asked, wrinkling her brow. "She just disappeared!"

"She has to be here somewhere," Randall Scott stated. "There aren't many places to hide up here."

The pair crept from rock to rock but could not find any sign of the old woman.

"It's impossible!" the professor insisted. "Where is she?"

Hiding between two boulders, they looked at each other in disbelief.

"There is only one explanation," Susan Sand firmly stated. "Randall, let's creep up to those two jagged rocks."

Without questioning Susan's motives, he followed her as she made her way silently toward the spot where Quentin Sutter had met his death. Just as they reached the protection of the huge boulders, they heard the old woman's voice muttering to herself. A moment later she appeared, seemingly from nowhere.

"They're gone! He's got them! The villain! Why did I wait?" she repeated over and over, the lantern swinging violently in her hand. Momentarily she stood looking about, swaying slightly. Then she started off down the trail. Randall Scott took several steps as if he intended to follow her, but Susan restrained him.

"No, Randall. She is most likely returning to the cottage. I think I know where she disappeared to."

Randall Scott looked at her, a puzzled expression on his handsome face. He watched as Susan hurried over to the two boulders and fell on her hands and knees.

"Randall! Come, quickly! Look what I've found!"

"Sue, what are you doing?" he queried.

"Look at this crevice," she said, pointing to a gap next to the two rocks. "This shrub hides it entirely. The earth tremor yesterday apparently caused the opening. The old woman must have climbed down into that little cave!"

"Why would she do that?" he asked.

Susan did not reply but was already letting herself down through the narrow gap. Randall Scott shined the flashlight into the opening and watched Susan drop to the bottom.

"The cave is much larger than I would have expected," she called up to him.

"Young lady, may I ask what you are doing?" he questioned, kneeling and peering into the cave.

"Looking for the Sutter jewels, just like the old woman," she replied. "Randall, don't you see?"

Quickly Randall Scott squeezed himself through the hole and dropped to the earth next to Susan Sand.

"There are the remains of Quentin Sutter's cape," said Susan, pointing to a rotted fragment that lay on the ground near their feet. "When the earthquake happened eighty years ago, and his cape got caught between those two boulders, he must have been carrying the Sutter jewels in the pocket. The cape was torn and the leather bag containing the gems dropped through the hole into this cave."

"But, Sue, if that is true, how would that old crone know where to look for them?"

"Randall, she must have been living here when that earthquake happened," Susan replied vehemently. "She has some connection with the Sutter family."

"And she returned here looking for the jewels!"

"Yes! No one would know about that cottage in the woods unless they had lived here before. But she isn't interested only in finding the jewels. She also knows something about Penelope. Think of how old she must be! Eighty years ago she would have been a teenager!"

"But she didn't find the jewels. We heard her say so herself!"

"No. Someone else did!"

"But who?"

"Dr. Coram!" Susan cried. "The tremor happened Saturday afternoon. He's had plenty of time to find them."

Professor Scott stood and thought for several moments, his eyes traveling around the cavern.

"Sue, no one knew that earth tremor was going to occur," he reasoned. "So why would the old crone be living in that cottage? She wouldn't be waiting for something that might never happen."

"That's a good point," Susan agreed. "Obviously she came back to Raggedrock Ridge for another reason. Penelope! When she looked in the window of Dudley House Saturday evening, she was looking for Penelope."

"The tremor made her think of the Sutter jewels and how she might find them!"

"It all makes sense," said Susan. "Randall, we must go back to the cottage and talk to her. I'm convinced she could tell us a great deal if we can only gain her confidence."

"I have to get my car," he reminded her.

"I don't think that we should try to see her at this hour," she stated, glancing at her watch. "It's four in the morning! We'll plan to return in the daylight."

"Sue, if Dr. Coram does have those jewels, how do you intend to find them?"

"Fortunately he has no idea that I overheard his conversation with Julia Leck and that we are suspicious of them. I'm living in Dudley House as a guest. What an opportunity to discover what he's done with the gems!"

Chapter XIII

Icky and Fussy

DAYLIGHT was already breaking through the early morning clouds when Susan Sand quietly turned the key and entered Dudley House. Randall Scott had headed back to Foxboro to the inn and planned to call her later in the morning when they had both had some sleep. As Susan started toward the stairs in the silent house, the sound of a voice made her jump.

"Sue!" called Marge, standing in the doorway of her room, balancing herself on the crutches. "Where have you been?"

Placing a finger on her lips, Susan hurried over to the redhead and motioned for her to return to her room.

"I don't want to wake anyone," she whispered, following Marge into the room and closing the door. "I have so much to tell you I don't know where to begin. I'm so glad you are awake!"

"That last time I saw you, you had fallen into a hole!" Marge said, sitting on the bed.

Susan laughed and threw herself into a big easy chair.

"I'm exhausted but it was worth it! Just listen to what we've discovered!" Quickly Susan related to her friend all that occurred since the previous afternoon.

"You found the old woman and the place where the Sutter jewels may have been lying for eighty years!" Marge exclaimed.

"Sssh!" Susan warned.

Suddenly there was a noise outside the room followed by a scratching sound.

"Icky!" Susan said, getting up and crossing to the door. "Come in!"

His fluffy tail sticking straight up, the marmalade cat stalked into the bedroom and emitted a loud yowl.

"It's too early for breakfast," replied his mistress, picking him up.

"But, Sue, how did that old lady get out of the cave?" Marge queried.

"Probably the same way we did," Susan replied. "She is remarkably agile. There is a shrub to grab on to growing right next to the crevice, and the rocks give one a foothold. It is possible that she never went down into the cave at all but just looked with her lantern."

"Then if Dr. Coram has the jewels, he must have them here in Dudley House!" Marge reasoned. "Poor Penelope! She has no idea her step-father is a criminal!"

"It is very sad for her," Susan said softly. "She will have to learn the truth sometime. That is why I must discover her identity! Perhaps her real parents are still alive."

"Dr. Coram and Julia Leck are a dangerous pair," Marge stated. "Imagine pushing Miss Bingham down the cellar stairs! She might have been killed! Why would they go to such lengths in order to have Dr. Coram adopt Penelope?"

"Randall and I are going to return to the cottage in the woods and question the old woman," Susan told her friend. "I am convinced that she knows a great deal about her."

"Sue, where do you think Dr. Coram would hide those jewels?" Marge asked. "It would be foolish to bring them here to Dudley House unless he had a foolproof hiding place."

"If he did find them, I doubt that he would keep them for long," Susan surmised.

"You mean he would get rid of them through a fence?" Marge returned. "Oh, Sue, we can't let that happen! They belong to the Sutter family!"

"I'll leave you with the problem for several hours," the raven-haired girl replied, yawning. "I'm going to get some sleep before Randall calls. I promised Mr. Sutter that I would bring him over to see his library."

Susan Sand awoke at eleven o'clock and dressed hurriedly. First she called Arthur Sutter and made a date to bring Randall Scott to luncheon at one that afternoon. Next she phoned her friend at the Foxboro Inn and told him of the invitation.

"That's great, Sue!" he exclaimed. "I'm going to drive back to Thornewood and pick up some things I need. I'll come to Dudley House a little before one."

As Susan descended the stairs from the Tower Room, Miss Leck, dressed in her white nurse's uniform, approached her, smiling charmingly.

"Miss Sand! You're just the person I wanted to see. Do you recall that yesterday I asked you to tea at my house? How about this afternoon?"

"That would be lovely," Susan replied. "Mr. Sutter has invited Professor Scott and me to luncheon at one o'clock. Perhaps I could come to see you around five? Or would that be too late?"

"Five o'clock is fine," Miss Leck replied. "Dr. Coram has office hours today, usually until three. I'm anxious for you to meet Fussy!"

Miss Leck thrust a piece of paper in Susan's hand.

"I've written the instructions on how to get to my house," she explained.

"Thank you," replied Susan. "I'll be there by five."

Fingering the slip of paper, Susan went to Marge's room and knocked on the door.

"Come in!" came the response. "Sue! I have some things to tell you. Listen!"

"What is it, Marge?"

"A little while ago Dr. Coram changed the bandage on my ankle," she returned. "And there, sitting in the cabinet in his office was a leather pouch! He saw me looking at it and said that he kept marbles for the children to play with. But what if those are the Sutter jewels inside? Remember how in *The Purloined Letter* by Poe the letter in question is in plain view for the entire story?"

"I suppose it is possible," Susan agreed. "But somehow I don't think that Dr. Coram would take such a chance."

"I wish that I could get a look in that leather bag," Marge murmured. "I'm so curious!"

"Marge, don't go taking any risks," warned Susan Sand. "We don't want the doctor to know that we even suspect he might have the jewels."

"Perhaps the leather pouch is just a foil to divert attention," Marge continued, undaunted. "Maybe he's hidden them in the grandfather clock in the hall. In at least two of the Nancy Drew stories something vital is hidden in a clock."

"Marge! If we look for the jewels, we must have some idea where to begin! Please don't place yourself in a dangerous position!"

"But I'm here alone in the house except for Miss Greenway, and she often goes out to do the shopping. Penelope is at school. What an opportunity!"

Susan Sand frowned doubtfully at her friend.

"I've been invited to tea at Miss Leck's" she said, showing her the piece of paper.

"Talk about danger! Miss Leck is about as safe as a cobra! Are you going?"

"Of course! Miss Leck doesn't know it yet, but I intend to bring Icky."

"Why do that, Sue?"

"Because I want to see how she reacts to him," Susan explained. "The first time she saw him she ran out of the house!"

"That was certainly peculiar," Marge murmured.

"There must have been a good reason for her to act like that when she loves cats and has one of her own," Susan said.

"When are you going to visit the old woman?" Marge asked. "I want to hear what she knows about Penelope."

"That will have to wait until tomorrow," Susan replied. "I can't turn down an opportunity to see Miss Leck."

Randall Scott arrived at the appointed time and Susan explained to him that she must take her own car, since she intended to drive to Miss Leck's at five. He showed great concern at her visiting the nurse but nothing he said could make her change her plans. When they reached Mr. Sutter's, the millionaire greeted them and Icky effusively and showed them into his study, a room that Susan had not yet seen.

"I've brought you in here, Susan, because yesterday I neglected to show you these pictures of the Sutter family," he explained, waving his arm at an array of old photographs on the wall. "This one is of Christopher just before the earthquake."

"Oh, how interesting!" Susan cried. "He looks about a year old. Who is that girl in the picture with him?"

"She must have been his nurse," Mr. Sutter replied. "I have no idea of her name. There were so many servants back in those days."

"I am delighted to have an opportunity to talk to you, Mr. Sutter," Professor Scott said cordially. "Have you ever considered writing a history of the Sutter family?"

Arthur Sutter seemed rather embarrassed at the suggestion.

"Well, I have given the idea some thought," he admitted. "But I am not a professional writer or historian."

"That doesn't matter," the professor assured him. "You know more about the Sutters than anyone else."

The subject was discussed during lunch and by the end of the meal Mr. Sutter was considerably excited over the project.

"A student of mine, Brian Lorenzo, might be interested in helping you with the research," Randall Scott suggested. "His field is American history, as is mine. I will contact him to see if he has time to assist you."

"Brian is a special friend of Marge's," said Susan. "I'm certain that he would want to know about her mishap, too."

"I'll call him as soon as I return to the inn," Professor Scott decided.

The afternoon passed quickly. Icky dined on shrimp and seemed noticeably fatter. After lunch Randall Scott and Arthur Sutter became engrossed in looking over the books in the library.

"Icky, I think it is time that you and I started for Miss Leck's," said Susan, picking him up.

Thanking Mr. Sutter for a pleasant luncheon, Susan left the pair discussing some aspect of the Sutter family and drove to Julia Leck's house. The dwelling was located about halfway to the Wayside Orphanage and Susan had no difficulty in finding the road.

"We have to keep our wits about us," she warned her pet, stepping from the car. "Now, don't get into a fight with Fussy!"

Fussy was a large, Maltese animal who was extremely suspicious at having a strange cat as a guest.

"He's used to receiving all the attention," said Miss Leck, offering Susan a chair.

Susan sat down and studied her hostess. Contrary to the previous day, Icky did not bother Julia Leck at all but raced off through the house after Fussy.

"What could have fascinated him so yesterday at Dudley House?" Susan asked herself. "He wouldn't leave Miss Leck alone!"

Julia Leck was a gracious hostess, serving lovely little cakes and delicious Chinese tea in tiny cups decorated with an Oriental design. She chatted amiably about the local people and Marge's mishap.

"It certainly is difficult to believe that she is a dangerous person," Susan thought, leaning back in her chair. "Could she really have pushed Miss Bingham down the stairs and shoved me into that hole on the ridge? It seems impossible!"

"I hope your friend's ankle heals soon," Miss Leck said, pouring Susan another cup of tea. "She must be very restless at being incapacitated."

"Yes, but she is enjoying her stay at Dudley House, as I am," Susan replied. "Penelope is an interesting companion and the doctor has been very kind."

Julia Leck smiled and took a bite out of her cake.

"Dudley is a kind man," she agreed. "I have worked for him for many years."

"Then you must know him very well," Susan answered.

"Yes, he is really more a friend than an employer. He has been wonderful to Penelope."

At that moment there was a loud crash from the kitchen. Susan and Miss Leck jumped from their chairs and rushed into the other room. A chair had been knocked over and both cats were up on a shelf, pawing at a small canister that had been pushed on its side, its contents spilled out.

"The catnip!" Miss Leck cried, running to the shelf and grabbing the container. Icky and Fussy were standing in the loose catnip, batting at each other with pieces of the herb falling from their paws.

"What a terrible thing to do!" Julia Leck shouted, grasping Fussy and almost throwing him to the floor. Icky received the same treatment and then the woman began to gather together the scattered catnip.

"Imagine! What a mess! What bad cats!" Miss Leck almost shrieked. "Miss Sand, why don't you go back to the living room. Your tea will be getting cold. I'll clean this up."

"Let me help you," Susan offered, crossing over to the shelf.

"No, no!" Julia Leck cried, shoving the top onto the canister. "I'll do it. You go back inside."

Susan Sand said nothing but returned to her chair in the living room.

"Why should she be so upset over such a small accident?" she asked herself. "And why did she want to get me out of the kitchen? She put the top back on before all the catnip was collected. Could there be something in that canister that she didn't want me to see?"

Chapter XIV

Return to the Cottage

"WHAT BAD CATS!" Julia Leck repeated, returning from the kitchen. "I must not have replaced the lid tightly. The catnip will be tracked all over the house."

Icky and Fussy, more excited than ever over their find, were chasing each other through the upstairs bedrooms.

"The catnip has gone to their heads!" Susan replied, laughing. "Perhaps it was a mistake to bring Icky with me."

"Oh, I'm glad you brought him," Miss Leck assured her, regaining her composure. "I'll make some more tea, nice and hot."

"Please don't," Susan insisted. "I left Randall Scott at Mr. Sutter's and I promised the professor that I would meet him back at Dudley House. I really should be going, provided I can catch Ikhnaton!"

"Ikhnaton! Such an imaginative name! Oh, here he comes now."

Icky, followed closely by Fussy, flew down the stairs, and onto the back of the couch where Julia Leck was sitting. He took one swipe at her head with a furry paw and sped on into the kitchen.

"They'll be at the catnip again!" Miss Leck cried, jumping up and running after them.

Susan followed her hostess and soon managed to capture her pet.

"We really must leave before any more damage is done," Susan said. "Thank you, Miss Leck, for the lovely tea and cakes. Perhaps sometime you can come to Thornewood to visit my aunt and me."

Once in her car, Susan Sand plopped Icky on the seat and looked at him affectionately.

"You did a fine job of sleuthing, Ikhnaton," she told him, stroking his head. "There is definitely something important in that canister of catnip. But what could it be?"

During the ride back to Dudley House, Susan pondered the question. As she started up the winding drive, she was delighted to see Randall Scott's car parked in front of the door. Entering the living room, the girl was greeted by Penelope, Miss Greenway, and Marge. Dr. Coram called a cheery hello from his seat by the fire, and Professor Scott crossed the room and took Icky from her. Susan related the episode at Miss Leck's and the entire party laughed heartily over the antics of the two cats and the catnip canister.

"Dr. Coram is certainly playing the part of a

gracious host," Susan told herself, looking thoughtfully at the doctor. "Are the jewels really here in Dudley House?"

"I'm glad you had an opportunity to get to know Julia better," he said smoothly, stroking his moustache. "She has raved to me about your detective stories. We both think very highly of them."

"Thank you, Dr. Coram," Susan answered, glancing at Randall Scott. "Did the professor tell you that Mr. Sutter is considering writing a history of the Sutter family?"

"Yes, he has just been talking to us about the project," the doctor replied. "A grand idea. I approve highly. Arthur needs something to occupy his mind. His heart condition prevents him from too much physical exertion."

"Isn't it a shame that no one ever found the Sutter jewels," said Marge boldly. "Where do you think they could be after all these years?"

"It's impossible to know," returned the doctor. "No one is going to find them now, Miss Halloran."

Susan turned a warning glance on her red-headed friend, and Marge said nothing further.

"I haven't yet been to Raggedrock Ridge," said Randall Scott untruthfully.

"You should ride up there," Dr. Coram said.

"Yes, Professor," added Penelope. "Father, why not let Susan and the professor take two of the horses and ride up the trail?"

"That is the best way to see the ridge," Miss Greenway agreed.

"Of course, take two horses," Dr. Coram offered. "George will saddle them for you. But it is best to go in the morning."

"Tomorrow will be fine," Randall Scott replied. "Thank you, Dr. Coram, for the offer of the horses. I'm a great riding fan, although I haven't had much chance to ride recently. People in this area are very hospitable. Mr. Sutter has offered to have me as a houseguest."

"How kind of him," Susan remarked.

"Brian is coming to see me," said Marge, flushing. "Isn't that great, Sue! He said he would be happy to help Mr. Sutter with his history."

"Wonderful! When are you expecting him?"

"Tomorrow morning," Penelope replied. "I asked him to stay with us, too, but he said that he has too much to do at the university to remain here."

Dr. Coram invited Randall Scott to dinner. During the meal, Susan smiled to herself over the doctor's performance.

"We are both acting," she thought. "Only he doesn't know that I suspect him! What a peculiar situation!"

The next morning Randall Scott, after having spent the night at Arthur Sutter's, arrived early for the ride up to the ridge. George Reger had saddled two horses and stood holding the reins as Susan and Randall approached the stables.

"Good morning, Mr. Reger," said Susan, climbing into the saddle.

"Mornin'," he replied. "Nice day for a ride."

As Susan Sand was about to urge her horse forward, she noticed an old battered lantern lying in a corner of the stables.

"Mr. Reger, that lantern looks exactly like the antique in the foyer at Dudley House," Susan remarked. "I should think that Dr. Coram would want to shine it up. They would make a nice pair."

"I never thought of that," the groom replied. "Except that this lantern is so dented and rusty, I don't think much could be done with it. It's been lying in that corner long as I can remember."

"Perhaps Penelope would be interested in it. I must tell her," Susan said.

Bidding good-bye to the groom, the pair started toward the trail that led to the summit of the ridge.

"Sue, I'm glad of the opportunity to talk to you alone," Randall Scott stated, bringing his horse alongside her mare. "Tell me about your visit at Miss Leck's."

Susan repeated the incident of the catnip canister and her suspicions about the nurse.

"Randall, I am beginning to get an idea about that canister and how it relates to Icky's unusual interest in Miss Leck Sunday afternoon."

"You mean the scent of catnip, don't you?" he reasoned.

"Exactly! I think Icky smelled catnip on Julia

Leck and that is the reason he wouldn't leave her alone.''

"Of course, Sue!" the professor cried. "That makes sense!"

"What if she kept something in that canister that was very important to her," Susan continued. "And for some reason she was carrying that object on Sunday, under her dress. Icky would immediately scent the herb and where it was."

"There are a lot of threads to this mystery," he mused. "I am anxious to find the old crone again."

"We'll ride to the top of the ridge and down the other side," Susan suggested. "That way, if anyone is watching us, they won't suspect where we are really going."

"I hope she will talk to us," the professor added. "Somehow I think she knows a great deal."

When they reached the summit, they rode over to the spot where the night before the old woman had looked for the Sutter jewels. Even in the daylight, the crevice was difficult to find.

"No one would ever think of searching for the gems here unless they believed the story of the kidnapping," Susan surmised. "I wonder if Dr. Coram really did find them?"

"The crone certainly thinks so," he replied.

"I'm concerned about Marge," Susan told him. "She has it in her head to search for the jewels when she is alone in the house. I hope she doesn't get into trouble!"

The pair rode down the other side of the ridge and into the woods. Fairly certain of their direction, they continued deeper into the forest and managed to find a narrow trail that had been made by previous riders. On horseback the distance did not seem so far as it had at night on foot, and soon the clearing came into view. In the light the little cottage looked forlorn and vacant, but as Susan and Randall Scott approached, the door opened and the old woman emerged, carrying a broom. She began to sweep the steps vigorously.

"She obviously considers the place her home," the professor remarked.

"Let's dismount here," Susan suggested. "Perhaps if we approach her slowly and on foot we won't frighten her as much."

Tying their horses to a tree, they started slowly toward the cottage. At first the old crone did not look up, but suddenly, becoming aware of their presence, she turned her head and stared directly at them. The broom clattered from her hand.

"Don't be frightened," Susan said softly. "I'm Susan Sand and this is my friend, Randall Scott. We must talk to you."

"How did you find me?" she croaked.

"We saw the smoke from your chimney," Susan explained.

"I was foolish but it gets cold here in the woods at night," she replied. "I had to light a fire. Well, now that you've found me, I suppose you'll tell Mr. Sutter."

"No, you have to trust us," Susan answered. "We promise not to tell anyone if only you will talk to us. Why were you looking in the window at Penelope the other night?"

The old woman did not reply but stood on the steps, twisting her apron in her fingers. Susan noticed that the tip of her left forefinger was missing. Her expression was forlorn and her black eyes looked pleadingly at them.

"It's been a long time since I talked to anyone," she said solemnly. "Penelope is all that matters now. Perhaps it is just as well that you found me."

"What is your name?" Susan asked, advancing toward the crone.

"I used to be known as Nanny Maud," she replied.

"Nanny Maud?" Susan repeated. "Were you a baby nurse?"

"Yes. Many years ago. If you would like to come inside, I'll make some coffee and tell you the story."

"Yes, we would like that," Susan answered. "I want to hear what you have to say. We've been looking for you, Nanny."

The old woman smiled sadly and ushered the pair into the cottage. Her meager belongings were arranged neatly and the room was immaculately clean. Silently, Nanny Maud began to set two places at a table that stood by one of the front windows. She shuffled back and forth from a cupboard to the table while Susan Sand and

Randall Scott watched from two wooden chairs where they had seated themselves.

"I know who you are, Miss Sand," she finally said. "I saw your picture in the paper and I've read *The Musty Trunk*. You're clever. I think that you can help me and Penelope."

"I would like to try, Nanny," Susan assured her.

"You just make yourselves comfortable," she said. "I'll go out into the kitchen and put on the coffee."

Nanny Maud retreated through a door, closing it behind her.

"Randall, what luck to find her!" Susan whispered. "She knows a great deal, probably enough to solve the entire mystery!"

"She certainly knows who Penelope is," he replied. "And she means a great deal to her."

Susan and Randall sat patiently as the minutes passed. Several times they could hear sounds from the back of the cottage as the old woman prepared the repast. When ten minutes had elapsed and she did not return, Susan rose and crossed over to the door where Nanny Maud had gone. Opening it a crack, she looked through into the other room.

"There's no one here," she said in alarm. "The back door is open!"

Rushing through the kitchen to the rear entrance, with Randall Scott closely at her heels, Susan Sand bent down and pointed to an over-turned milk container that lay just outside.

"I'm afraid something has happened to her!" Susan exclaimed.

"She would never run away," the professor said. "She wanted to talk to us."

"Look! Over there in the woods!" cried Susan. "Isn't that her scarf? Oh, Randall, maybe she's been kidnapped!"

Chapter XV

An Old Photograph

"THAT IS HER SCARF," Randall Scott replied, hurrying over to a piece of blue cloth that lay near a huge oak tree. "She was wearing it around her neck when we arrived."

Picking the scarf up, the young professor stood thoughtfully turning it over in his hand.

"There's a very faint trail," said Susan Sand, taking his arm. "Hurry, Randall, perhaps we can find her!"

Susan started off down the narrow path, keeping her eyes on the ground for further clues. There was no evidence of footprints, for the weather had been dry and the earth was covered with October leaves. After about a quarter of a mile, Susan gave a cry and dashed over to a black object that lay off to one side of the path.

"A shoe!" she called triumphantly to Randall Scott. "She *was* brought in this direction. If she ran away of her own accord, she wouldn't leave a shoe behind!"

Susan picked up the shoe and continued on down the trail. In another quarter of a mile the road widened suddenly and the trees thinned.

"Tire tracks!" Susan pointed out to her companion. "How unfortunate! A car could be miles away by now."

"These tracks look recent," Randall Scott said, kneeling down.

"I doubt that there would be many cars out here," Susan surmised. "Unfortunately, there are no clear tread marks. We're at a dead end!"

Dejectedly the pair turned back and walked slowly down the trail toward the old crone's cottage.

"Perhaps a search of her belongings will give us some lead," Susan said hopefully.

"How are we ever going to find her?" the young professor asked. "We don't know who the kidnapper or kidnappers are and we have no way of knowing where she might have been taken."

"She may very well have enemies," Susan reasoned. "We haven't learned anything about her except what she told us."

"Which isn't much," Randall added.

"She said she was known as Nanny Maud and that Penelope was all that mattered now," Susan recalled. "She really wanted to talk to us. Randall, could we have been followed from Dudley House?"

"I thought of that," he replied. "Sue, what if Dr. Coram is responsible for this."

"He knew we were out riding, but had he discovered Nanny Maud?'' she wondered aloud. ''Or did we lead him to her?''

''Perhaps he's acquainted with her from the past,'' he suggested. ''The old woman was certain who took those jewels. I'm inclined to think the doctor is behind all of it.''

When the pair reached the cottage they made a thorough search of Nanny Maud's belongings. There was an old canvas bag in the bedroom but no personal identification of any kind.

''Look,'' Susan said, holding up a small gold chain. ''This is probably the chain we saw through the window the other night. It seemed to mean a great deal to her. See, here in the middle? Something has been broken off.''

''Yes, it looks as though part of it has been lost,'' Randall Scott noted. ''Why should a simple piece like this mean so much to her?''

Susan replaced the chain and continued to search. In the kitchen the coffee was boiling away on the potbellied stove. Susan removed the pot, retrieved the milk from outside and closed the back door. On the table was a shopping list in old-fashioned, spidery handwriting. Impulsively, she slipped the paper into her pocket.

''There is nothing here to give us any idea where she might be,'' Randall Scott said, downcast. ''What do we do now, Sue?''

''We go to Arthur Sutter's,'' Susan replied.

''Arthur Sutter's? Why there? You're not going to tell him about this?''

''No, of course not. But I want to get another

look at the picture he showed us. Remember the old photograph of the baby Christopher? There was a young nurse holding him. I have an idea about that picture.''

After closing up the cottage Susan Sand and Randall Scott returned to their horses and rode back to Mr. Sutter's mansion.

"He has a visitor," the professor said, pointing out a car that was parked nearby.

"I must see that photograph," Susan insisted. "Since you are now his houseguest, an unannounced visit won't appear rude."

"I must tell him that Brian Lorenzo is arriving today," he replied. "He's anxious to meet him."

"For the time being, we shall say nothing about what has happened," Susan stated. "Nanny Maud was beginning to trust us, and until we find her I don't want to reveal that she was living in Mr. Sutter's cottage."

Mr. Sutter greeted them cordially and invited them to have coffee. In the living room, they were surprised to see Esther Greenway seated on the couch. Arthur Sutter appeared to be elated over her visit.

"I do believe that he is very interested in Miss Greenway," Susan thought, smiling to herself. "How nice if a romance is in the offing!"

"I'm so happy that Arthur is going to write a history of the Sutter family," Esther Greenway remarked. "He's needed an important project to keep him occupied. Just think of all the research involved! Why, Arthur, it could take years!"

"With two young men from Irongate University helping me, I might become a famous historian!" he replied, laughing.

"Penelope is delighted," Miss Greenway replied. "She's always been fond of you, Arthur."

"Pen is a wonderful girl," the millionaire said. "She's lucky to have had you all these years, Esther. . . . You've been like a mother to her."

"I have always felt that she was my own daughter," she returned. "She has been lonesome living out here in the country. I'm grateful to you, Susan, for bringing some excitement into her life!"

"Marge and Penelope get along so well," Susan answered. "I suspect that they will become fast friends. So, you see, the earth tremor was a fortunate occurrence, after all!"

"Pen has always been bothered by not knowing who her real parents were," Arthur Sutter divulged. "I have talked to her about it several times. She is a sensitive girl, and even though Dudley has been kind to her, he is not like a real father."

"He has tried," Esther Greenway offered. "But it isn't easy for a bachelor to bring up a child. When he hired me, he told me he wanted to give her as normal a life as possible. Essentially she has been happy."

Susan and Randall listened closely to the conversation but gave no indication that they suspected Dr. Coram of wrongdoing. Until they uncovered hard facts and could prove something against the doctor, the matter had to remain a secret.

As the conversation continued, Susan managed to slip into the study. The photograph of Christopher Sutter and his young nurse hung on the wall near a window. Quickly Susan studied the old print.

"Her hand!" she gasped. "The tip of her left forefinger is missing! Just like Nanny Maud's! What a discovery! My hunch was correct. Nanny Maud was Christopher Sutter's nurse!"

Chapter XVI

A Piece of Paper

"SO THAT'S WHERE you disappeared to," said Randall Scott, standing in the doorway of Arthur Sutter's study. "What are you doing, Sue?"

"Just taking another look at these old photographs," Susan Sand answered casually. "They are very interesting."

"I was telling Mr. Sutter and Miss Greenway that we should be getting back to Dudley House to meet Brian Lorenzo. He was due to arrive this morning."

"Of course," Susan agreed, crossing the room and glancing at her watch. "It's past one o'clock!"

"I'm anxious to meet the young man," Arthur Sutter said, escorting them to the front door. "Bring him over as soon as you can."

"I understand that he is a friend of Marge's," Miss Greenway offered.

"Yes. They have known each other for several years," Susan replied. "I know he will be concerned over her accident."

After saying good-bye, Susan and Randall returned to their horses and started back through the woods. As soon as they were safely out of earshot, Susan told him of her discovery.

"Sue!" he exclaimed. "If Nanny Maud is the girl in that picture, that means she was probably the kidnapper of Christopher! You're certain about the finger?"

"Positive. I specifically noticed her hand this morning when she was setting the table. And, Randall, there was something else in that print. Christopher Sutter was wearing a chain around his neck."

"You mean with the little ring attached that Mr. Sutter told you about?"

"Yes. I would never be certain what it was if I didn't know that the Sutter babies wore such jewelry. Randall, perhaps the chain we found in the cottage among Nanny Maud's belongings was once worn by Christopher Sutter."

"That is a possibility. Something had been broken off the middle," he mused.

"If that were true, it looks more than ever as if Nanny Maud kidnapped Christopher Sutter!" Susan rejoined.

"Then why was she herself kidnapped?" he responded.

"We are never going to find the answer to that

until we find her," Susan said. "It's so frustrating to have her snatched away just when she was going to talk to us!"

"It is also very puzzling," Randall Scott replied. "There is certainly a great deal that we don't know."

The pair rode on in silence until they reached the cottage where Nanny Maud had taken up residence. Susan drew her mare to a halt and jumped to the ground.

"What are you doing, Sue?" her companion asked.

"I want to get that chain," she answered, going into the cottage. "I have a feeling it is an important part of this mystery."

In a few moments she returned, the chain dangling from her hand.

"This piece is a real clue," she said, slipping it into her pocket. "And we need plenty of them right now!"

"What's our next move?" Randall Scott asked. "We're at a dead end."

"I was thinking about returning to see Miss Bingham," she revealed, urging her horse forward. "We promised her that we would keep her informed. After all, she was very helpful, telling us about Penelope and her suspicion of Miss Leck."

"I don't see how it will advance us very much," Randall said skeptically.

"No. But I would like to ask Miss Bingham if we could see Penelope's folder."

"You mean the file that was kept on her when she was left at the orphanage," he queried.

"Yes. Perhaps there is something in that folder that will give us a lead."

"Do you want to go to the orphanage now?" Randall Scott inquired.

"As soon as possible," Susan replied. "First I think we should return the horses to the Dudley stables, and I would like to see Brian. He must wonder where we are."

Brian Lorenzo's car was parked in front of Dudley House when Susan and Randall arrived. George Reger took the reins from the two riders, and they hurried into the house to greet their friend.

Brian Lorenzo was an extremely tall, lean young man with curly black hair and lively black eyes. Marge, her freckled face beaming, looked happier than she had since the accident had incapacitated her.

"Well, it's about time you two arrived!" Brian said impishly. "Professor, what have you and your sleuth-friend been up to?"

"Now, you behave yourself, Mr. Lorenzo," Randall Scott replied in mock severity. "After all, you are merely one of my students, and I am a very strict disciplinarian. I must keep you in line."

Penelope squealed in delight from her seat by the window.

"Have you been sleuthing today, Susan?" she asked.

Susan Sand wished that she could truthfully reply to the girl, but her position forced her to pretend that nothing was amiss. Until Dr. Coram could be revealed, she had to play the part of a gracious guest and protect her young hostess as much as possible.

"Have you ever heard about her work at Clovercrest Castle?" Brian asked.

"Never," Penelope rejoined. "Tell us about it, Susan!"

Susan Sand cast an annoyed glance at Brian.

"You know I don't like to discuss my previous cases," she reprimanded him. "Marge, you are going to have to learn to control him!"

Marge flushed becomingly.

"No one can control me!" Brian answered in a boasting tone. "Least of all, Miss Freckle-face!"

"But Susan, you did say you wanted to solve the mystery of the Sutter jewels," Penelope insisted.

"Penelope, please stop bothering our guest," said Dr. Coram, entering the room and seating himself by his adopted daughter.

"I'm sorry," Penelope returned. "I thought Susan was interested."

"Oh, Penelope, I am interested," Susan said, her heart warming toward the girl.

"What is all this about the Sutter jewels?" Brian asked innocently. "It sounds intriguing."

"I'll tell you about it later, Brian," said Marge, looking at the doctor's darkening face. "Right now, I think you should ask Professor Scott about Mr. Sutter and his project."

"That's why I came," the young man replied, grinning. "When can I meet him?"

"He's waiting to see you," Randall Scott answered. "We can go over right now."

"Oh, may I come?" Marge asked. "I've been in so long, a trip would be exciting!"

"I see no reason why you shouldn't go," Dr. Coram offered. "As long as you don't put weight on your ankle."

"I would like to go, too," Penelope interjected. "I haven't seen Mr. Sutter in ages."

Fifteen minutes later the small party set out in Professor Scott's car for the Sutter Mansion. Susan, saying she had something to look up at the Foxboro Library, started in her own car for the Wayside Orphanage. In case Dr. Coram decided to follow her, or have Julia Leck do so, she made a short visit to the library before driving on to the orphanage, where Miss Bingham greeted her cordially.

"I'm very glad to see you again, Miss Sand," she said, bringing her to her office. "I've done a great deal of thinking about our conversation Sunday night."

"I have something important to tell you," Susan began, seating herself by the administrator's desk. "And I have a request."

Briefly, the raven-haired girl told Miss Bingham about the discovery of Nanny Maud and her subsequent identity.

"Christopher Sutter's nurse!" the woman cried, dumbfounded. "She would have to be at least ninety-five! And you think that she kidnapped the baby at the time of the earthquake?"

"Everything points in that direction," Susan replied. "But we can't understand why anyone would want to kidnap her."

"How fascinating!" Miss Bingham uttered.

"Professor Scott and I wonder if Dr. Coram and Miss Leck are at the bottom of it," Susan said.

"It is very likely," Miss Bingham agreed. "Nanny Maud must know something that they want to keep quiet. If they are behind it, what a shock they must have had to learn that she was still alive!"

"Miss Bingham, would it be possible for me to see the file on Penelope?" Susan asked. "I was hoping it might give me a lead, however slim."

"I have no objection to showing it to you, Susan," Miss Bingham replied, rising from behind her desk. "I am afraid you will be disappointed, though. I have studied that file myself. All it contains is the original form that I filled out when Penelope was left here, along with her fingerprints and footprints."

The administrator left the office and returned five minutes later, the folder in her hand. As soon as she placed the file on her blotter, the orphanage cat, who had been sleeping in a basket in the corner, awakened and started to meow loudly.

"What is it, Casper?" Miss Bingham asked. "Are you hungry this early?"

"No, it's the folder!" Susan exclaimed. "He's heading straight for the folder!"

"Why on earth would he do that?" the administrator wondered.

Casper had jumped onto the desk and was pushing his nose vigorously into the manila file folder. Opening it, Miss Bingham looked puzzled.

"What is this?" she said, picking up a small piece of yellowed paper that lay on top. Casper made a lunge toward it and tried to grab it with his teeth.

"Susan, look at this!" said Miss Bingham, thrusting the paper into her hand.

Susan Sand took the paper and read the words aloud.

"This child is Penelope Sutter, the granddaughter of Christopher Sutter. She will be one year old on June 11,"

the old-fashioned handwriting said.

"How incredible!" Miss Bingham gasped. "Susan, that note was not in the folder just a short time ago. Someone placed it there!"

"I think I know where it was," Susan replied, quickly telling the administrator about the catnip canister in Julia Leck's kitchen.

"Then Julia Leck and Dr. Coram have known all these years about Penelope's identity and have kept it a secret!" Miss Bingham reasoned.

"Miss Leck kept this vital piece of paper in the catnip canister," Susan continued. "She must have become worried about it after my arrival, so she carried it with her the day Icky pawed at her waist so vigorously. She must have had it pinned to the inside of her dress."

"But why would she put it in the folder now, and where did she find it in the first place?"

"This handwriting is Nanny Maud's," Susan said, comparing the spidery scrawl with that on the shopping list she had found in the cottage in the woods. "She must have left the note in the basket with Penelope to make it clear just who she was, and somehow Dr. Coram or Julia Leck or both found the baby."

"The date and time are written in the corner," Miss Bingham noted. "They coincide exactly with the night I found Penelope on the doorstep."

"All these years they have known who Penelope is," Susan said. "No wonder Dr. Coram was so anxious to adopt her! He's been planning to get the Sutter money!"

"Susan, I must go to the authorities over this," Miss Bingham said authoritatively. "It is a matter for the police."

"I agree with you," Susan answered. "But please give me time to try to find Nanny Maud. There is no way of proving that Dr. Coram and Julia Leck are guilty. That is why the note was put in the folder. They will deny ever knowing anything about it. Only Nanny Maud herself can establish their culpability. Unless we find her, they may never be brought to justice!"

Chapter XVII

Susan's Search

"SUSAN, if your reasoning is correct," Miss Bingham said, "why would Dr. Coram and Julia Leck decide to put the note in Penelope's file? Why wouldn't they destroy it instead?"

"Because I suspect that Dr. Coram, after bringing up Penelope all these years, still has hopes of getting some of the Sutter money. He will deny knowing who the girl is, but he did adopt her. Julia Leck is extremely clever to rid herself of that incriminating piece of paper so quickly."

"This puts me into a serious situation," Miss Bingham replied, sitting down and looking at the file folder. "It is my word against theirs that the paper was not here. Dr. Coram is a respected physician who has been coming to the orphanage for many years. Why should the authorities believe me and not him?"

"That is why I must find Nanny Maud!" Susan said vehemently.

"But, Susan," replied the administrator. "She

could be miles away from here by now. Where would you begin such a search?''

"It does seem an impossible task," Susan rejoined, stroking Casper, who was still trying to get the catnip-scented piece of paper.

"Did you find any clues to give you an idea where she might have been taken?"

"Her scarf was lying not far from the back door of the cottage," Susan replied. "But farther on down the trail we found one of her shoes. Then we came to a place where the trail widens into a road. There were tire tracks, so we assumed she was driven off in a car."

"There is a road that eventually leads to the highway. I'm afraid the police are the only ones to conduct a search of this kind," Miss Bingham concluded. "Yet if I contact them, and the old woman is not found, Dr. Coram and Miss Leck will slip out of the net! Susan, what are we to do?"

"My first move should be to return to the site of the kidnapping," Susan decided. "Professor Scott and I didn't spend much time looking over the area. Perhaps a thorough investigation will yield some new evidence."

"How odd that Nanny Maud would move into one of those old cottages," Miss Bingham mused. "Whatever gave her such an idea?"

"It was really an intelligent thing to do," Susan said. "Only by chance did we see the smoke coming from the chimney. Otherwise, we probably never would have found her. By going back to the cottage she knew as a girl, she would be close to Penelope.''

''There is still so much we don't know,'' Miss Bingham rejoined angrily. ''If Nanny Maud had left the baby on our doorstep, the note would have been in the basket. Of that we can be certain.''

''I suspect that is where Dr. Coram and Julia Leck entered the picture,'' Susan continued. ''Somehow they found the baby.''

''This is nothing but guesswork, Susan. If only we could talk to that old woman!''

''While it is still daylight, I am going back to the woods,'' Susan decided, starting for the door.

''Be careful of those woods,'' Miss Bingham warned. ''I used to play there in the cottages as a child, and it is very easy to become lost, especially after dark.''

''How many cottages are there?'' Susan queried.

''Three, as I remember.''

''Please don't worry,'' Susan returned. ''I won't do anything foolish.''

The day had been clear and brisk, but as Susan Sand started toward the woods, a cold wind came up and gray, October clouds scudded across the sky. Approaching the forest, she became acutely aware of how vast it was and that to enter alone, with dusk approaching, was dangerous.

''At least Randall and I were together when we found Nanny Maud,'' Susan thought. ''But I have my compass and flashlight and I know the path that leads to the cottage.''

Driving to the spot where they had found the tire marks, Susan parked her car among the trees and began to search the area carefully. Standing on the edge of the woods and looking off into the distance, she could see a thin, gray ribbon of road.

"That must be the highway Miss Bingham spoke of," Susan decided. "If Nanny Maud was driven that way, I'm out of luck."

The tire marks seemed to lead to a paved road which led on to the highway, but Susan could not be certain that the car had gone in that direction. Walking on till she reached the beginning of the macadam, she adjusted her glasses and studied the ground.

"A car could have come the way I did just now and never approach this road," she reasoned. "What if Nanny Maud was taken back toward Foxboro? Perhaps an attempt was made to confuse us so that we would think the car had been driven off this way."

Susan stood for several moments and stared down the road toward the highway. Not a car was in sight, and she became more aware of how isolated Raggedrock Ridge was.

"I would think that days could go by without anyone coming this way," she decided, walking back toward the woods. "If I return to the cottage and look about there, maybe I will uncover something."

Susan was now thoroughly familiar with the path to the little house. As she advanced along it, she continued to study the ground in the hopes of stumbling upon new evidence. Although it was not quite five o'clock, she found that she needed her flashlight in order to see properly, for the trees grew thickly together. Many of them were pines and those that were shedding their leaves still provided a huge canopy overhead.

Because Susan continued to carefully scan the ground, her progress was slow. By the time she came upon the cottage, the sun was setting and a faint orange glow filtered dimly through the trees, lending an eerie atmosphere to the lonesome spot. Entering the little house, she sat down on one of the wooden chairs and contemplated her next move.

"Randall and I searched this place very well earlier," she thought. "I doubt that we overlooked anything."

Near the fireplace was the shoe that Susan had found on the trail and brought back. She had dropped it there before she and Professor Scott looked through the old woman's belongings.

"This is absolute proof that Nanny Maud did not go off on her own," Susan said to herself, crossing over to the fireplace and picking up the black shoe. "I'm certain she was kidnapped."

Replacing the shoe, Susan made another search of the small cottage but was unable to find a single new clue. Disheartened, she left the house and headed in another direction, playing the flashlight back and forth on the ground. A new idea was beginning to form in her mind and she started to walk faster.

"If I am right, it will be the first piece of luck in a long while," she thought. "But I musn't get lost! That would be disastrous!"

Susan Sand searched about for a hint of another trail, but the trees seemed to become thicker as she moved away from the cottage. Her instinct told her that she should follow her new thought, even if she was unsuccessful.

Pushing on through the woods, reading her compass all the while, Susan traveled in a southeasterly direction, deeper into the forest. There was no path whatsoever. By now, darkness had fallen and her flashlight was her only protection against total blackness.

"If these batteries give out, I am lost!" she realized. "But I'm fairly certain that I replaced them recently."

Ten minutes later, Susan cried out in delight, for her hunch had been rewarded. Directly in front of her was another cottage, almost identical to the one in which Nanny Maud had taken up residence, but in far greater need of repair. Instinctively, Susan crept forward like an Indian and peered through one of the windows.

"I can't see a thing. The cottage seems empty, but I must make sure."

Carefully, Susan approached the door and quietly opened it. Inside there was a scurrying sound as animals of the forest ran in every direc-

tion. Stepping across the threshold, Susan closed the door and turned her beam into the room. It was empty and there was no sign that anyone had been there for many years.

"If this cottage is like the other one, there should be a bedroom and a kitchen," Susan told herself, crossing over to another door and opening it. "Yes, this is the kitchen. Why, the roof is half fallen in and the stove has gone through the floor!"

Susan searched the room and continued on into the bedroom. As she opened the door, she thought that she heard a faint noise. A sudden fear gripped her and for a moment she wanted to run. Curiosity, however, took the upper hand, and she played the light over the walls. In one corner stood a bed, the covers piled in a heap in the middle. As Susan started toward it, the hump moved and then groaned! Quickly she crossed to the bed and threw back the blanket. Two bright black eyes looked up at her.

"Nanny Maud!" Susan exclaimed to the bound-and-gagged figure, immediately removing the cloth from her mouth.

"Those villains!" the old woman spat out. "You're a brave girl, Susan Sand. They might come back any minute. Just untie me and they'll be sorry!"

"You mean Dr. Coram and Julia Leck?"

"Of course! Who else? They kidnapped me. You didn't think I would run away, did you?"

"Oh, Nanny, I am so glad to find you!"

"No gladder than I am to be found!" the old crone cackled. "Now, you just listen to what I have to tell!"

Chapter XVIII

Nanny Maud's Explanation

"NANNY, I must get you out of here!" said Susan Sand, working at the knots that bound the old woman's wrists.

"Such cowards! Tying me up like a chicken!" Nanny Maud exclaimed. "How did you ever find me, Susan?"

"I had a hunch and it proved correct," Susan answered, feverishly picking at the thick ropes. "I knew that I was dealing with an extremely clever pair, and it occurred to me that perhaps a false trail had been laid to put me off the scent. Then I began to think about these cottages and what a good hiding place they would make because no one would suspect that they would put you here."

"No one but Susan Sand!" Nanny Maud replied. "When I went into the kitchen to make the coffee, the two of them were outside the back door. As soon as I opened it to get the milk, a hand was over my mouth and my hands were tied. Then they took me through the woods to this cottage. That Nurse Leck stayed with me, and Dr. Coram left but he came back later."

"He must have put your shoe on the trail to make me think you had been taken that way. Then he drove the car making the tire tracks."

"They want those jewels!" Nanny Maud whispered. "They think that I know where they are. I keep insisting that I don't, but they won't believe me."

"Then Dr. Coram didn't find them!" Susan surmised.

"No, he didn't!" the old woman cried. "I was certain I knew where to look, but when I went to the place, they weren't there! I thought he had gotten there before me, but I was wrong."

"Where could they be?" Susan wondered, finally freeing Nanny Maud's hands and starting on her feet.

"I've thought and thought and I don't know," she replied.

Susan worked diligently on the knots.

"There! You're free!" she cried triumphantly a few minutes later. "They weren't tied so tightly. Now hurry!"

"And me with only one shoe!" Nanny Maud lamented.

"I'll help you and we'll go to your cottage and get the other one. I put it there after I found it on the trail."

Nanny Maud's agility and strength amazed Susan. She hurried from the house and into the woods with the speed of a young girl, half hopping because of her missing shoe. Susan wanted to assist her, but she shook off any attempt to take her arm and insisted on making her own way.

"It's a good thing you have that flashlight," she said. "Otherwise we might be out here all night!"

With the aid of the compass, the pair reached Nanny Maud's cottage without any difficulty. Once inside, the old crone lighted a single lantern and pulled the ragged curtains across the windows.

"Just in case they get the idea to look here, I won't light any candles," she announced, retrieving her shoe. "We might just as well make ourselves at home."

"I have my car parked back at the beginning of the trail," Susan stated. "Perhaps, Nanny, we should get away from here and go back to Foxboro."

"Not on your life!" she squeaked. "What would I do? Check into the Foxboro Inn? He-he-he. What a joke that would be! Susan, everyone thinks that I've been dead for eighty years! That is, everyone around these parts does."

"Nanny, what did happen at the time of the earthquake?" Susan asked, looking earnestly at her. "You were Christopher Sutter's nurse, weren't you?"

"Yes, Susan, I was and just sixteen at the time," the old woman replied.

"I saw the picture of you and the baby at Mr. Sutter's. The missing fingertip gave you away."

"Ah, this finger," she replied, holding up her left hand. "I lost the tip of it in an accident. But, Susan, I am not guilty of kidnapping the child in the way you might think. Christopher Sutter was kidnapped by a man named James Benson."

"How do you know that?" Susan queried. "And if he took the baby, what happened to him?"

"He disappeared during the earthquake," she returned, walking over to the fireplace and lighting some kindling. "Goodness, it's cold out here at night!"

"Then how did you get the child and where have you been all these years?"

Nanny Maud sat down at the table and folded her gnarled hands on the cloth.

"Let me tell you the story from the beginning," she said, breathing deeply. "I must make you understand because, you see, I have been a fugitive from justice all this time."

"Nanny, before you start, I have to know one thing. Is Christopher Sutter still alive?"

"No, Susan, he isn't," she replied, wiping tears away from her black eyes. "He was killed in World War Two."

"Oh, I see," said Susan, sitting back in her chair. "Mr. Sutter had hoped that perhaps he was still alive. He knew that if he were, he would be unaware of his identity."

"Poor Mr. Sutter," Nanny Maud sighed. "I suppose I have been unfair to him through the years, but I had to be. I tried to do the right thing in the first place.

"At the time that I was Christopher's nurse, the Sutters were the wealthiest family in the entire state," she began. "Abigail, the mother, died when the child was born and Quentin, the father, was heartbroken. At least he had the baby and he loved it dearly. He used to say to me, 'Nanny, take good care of that baby. He's all I have.' Now that may sound strange when you think of all his money, but it was true, really. No one cared about that child except Quentin Sutter and me. Quentin's sister, Emily, was a snooty thing, interested only in her men friends and wanting nothing to do with a squawling baby. Changing diapers was not for her! So I became just like Christopher's mother.

"Then all the trouble started. One attempt was made to kidnap Christopher, but it was a clumsy try and the pair was caught and sent to jail. James Benson was a different proposition, and his girl friend, Doris Carver, was so stupid that she would do anything he wanted."

"Doris Carver and James Benson," repeated Susan. "Who were they, Nanny?"

"James Benson worked for Quentin Sutter and Doris Carver was a maid at Dudley House," she answered. "Because James was an insider at the Sutter Mansion, he had a perfect opportunity to plan the kidnapping. Quentin Sutter was completely fooled by him and trusted him. Benson wanted those jewels, so he worked on Doris Carver's affections and got her to help him.''

"You say that Doris Carver worked at Dudley House as a maid?''

"Yes. Back then there were many servants, and they all had different duties. Doris made the candles, did the washing, and a lot of other chores. But she was a greedy one and entirely in James Benson's power. I was suspicious of her from the beginning, but I had no idea she would be in on a kidnapping!

"On the day that it happened, I had been on a trip, and Christopher was left with that Emily, who paid no attention to him. Just before the earthquake, I arrived back at the Sutter Mansion late at night, and Christopher wasn't there! Emily came in and said she didn't know who had taken him. Quentin was not at home. I was in a panic. All I could think of was maybe James Benson and Doris Carver had something to do with his disappearance, so I took a lantern and headed for Dudley House. When I was halfway there the earthquake happened. Well, that changed everything! Never have I had such an experience, and to try and describe it would be impossible! It didn't last long, but the damage was extensive. I was one of the lucky ones and I wasn't even hurt, but there were many others who weren't so lucky. When I arrived at the Dudley stables, I was surprised to see that they were still standing, but that happened all over during the earthquake. Dudley House wasn't even touched by it.

"As I approached the stables, I heard a baby crying. I rushed inside and there was my precious Christopher all by himself in an old basket! The stables were empty but I could see that Doris had been making candles, for the stuff was all over the place and she had some candles out drying. But I couldn't find her. Then I noticed that the diamond-studded ring that all the Sutter babies wore had been broken off the chain around the baby's neck!"

"So you thought that Doris had stolen the ring," Susan reasoned. "But what happened to her? Where was she?"

"I still don't know to this day, but she must have been killed," Nanny Maud replied, stirring the fire with the poker. "She was never found and neither was James Benson, but it didn't take me long to figure out what must have occurred. I think that Benson took the baby and brought it to the stables for Doris to keep until he got the jewels as a ransom payment. He told Quentin Sutter that he had the baby and to bring the Sutter jewels up to Raggedrock Ridge. Quentin Sutter would never think twice about it, for he would do anything to get his baby back, so he took the jewels from the safe and rode up to the ridge to give them to James Benson. But fate intervened and the earthquake happened before Benson got his hands on those gems."

"Nanny, you can't be certain of any of this, can you?" Susan asked.

"No, not certain, but almost so," she replied. "Because after the earthquake it was discovered that the jewels were missing, so all I had to do was piece it together. At the time I didn't spend much time over it, because all I wanted to do was take Christopher away from his aunt Emily. As soon as I learned that Quentin Sutter was dead, I took the baby and left. Not a soul knew where he was, and no one was interested in me, anyway. There was such confusion I had no trouble escaping."

"All those years you lived somewhere else with Christopher Sutter?" Susan asked.

"Yes, Susan. I brought him up as my own child. As time passed, I realized more and more that I had really committed a criminal act, but I did it because there was no one else to take care of him! I knew that no one loved him the way I did, and Emily couldn't stand me and intended to have me fired."

"Did you give him your name?" Susan asked.

"Yes. He was known as Christopher Waverly. I told people that my husband was dead, and no one ever questioned it. I worked as a maid and Christopher grew up and married and had a child, a boy, Penelope's father. When Christopher was killed in the war, I was heartsick, but I still had his baby to care for. Years later, Penelope came along and I was happy to help take care of another baby but before she was ten months old, both her parents were killed in a tragic accident.

"I was really worried because I realized that someone had to care for her, and I was over eighty then, so I thought of Arthur Sutter. I decided to bring the baby to the Sutter Mansion and leave her there with a note telling who she was. If I appeared I might be prosecuted as a kidnapper! So I left the baby on the doorstep of the Sutter Mansion."

"But she was found at the Wayside Orphanage!" Susan cried.

"Yes, Susan," Nanny Maud replied. "Imagine the shock I had when I read in the papers about this beautiful red-haired baby being found on the doorsteps of the orphanage! I couldn't understand what had happened, but I was afraid to return; and then I read that Dr. Coram had adopted her, so I relaxed somewhat. But I knew that there was funny business somewhere.

"For fifteen years I wondered about Penelope, and a month ago I decided to come back just to see her. I had lived in this cottage when I was a nanny so I moved back in as if no time had passed! I couldn't be seen, but I took the chance of going to Dudley House that night you saw me looking in the window. I knew you had spotted me but what could I do? I recognized you from your pictures and thought if I talked to you, maybe I could find out why my Penelope was not living at the Sutters where she should be."

"Nanny, it was Julia Leck who had that note you left with Penelope," Susan told her. "Somehow she and Dr. Coram found the baby where you placed her outside the Sutter Mansion. Apparently they planned to get the Sutter money someday by having Dr. Coram adopt Penelope."

"Such treachery! They want the money and the jewels! But James Benson must have escaped with them back at the time of the earthquake or else they would have been up there on the ridge where Quentin was killed. After the earth tremor on Saturday I thought about those jewels and how maybe there was a way of finding them. It occurred to me that the tremor might have done enough damage to cause some new cracks. But the jewels weren't where I thought they would be. I decided Dr. Coram must have discovered them, but now I wonder if James Benson hadn't already received them when the earthquake happened."

"You said that James Benson was never found," Susan replied.

"No. I followed the newspapers diligently at the time and no mention was ever made of him. He must have taken the jewels and continued on his horse."

"But, Nanny," Susan said, wrinkling her brow and adjusting her glasses. "James Benson wouldn't have had time to escape if the earth started to shake right after he received the jewels from Quentin Sutter. Didn't Raggedrock Ridge suffer the most damage?"

"Yes, the ridge took the brunt of the quake," Nanny Maud replied thoughtfully.

"Then maybe the jewels are still up there but in a different spot from where Quentin Sutter was killed," Susan excitedly rejoined.

"I never thought of that!" Nanny Maud answered. "I decided that he had escaped, but you could be right. Maybe he was killed, too, only he fell into a hole with the jewels and disappeared!"

"Let's look for them, Nanny!" Susan said decisively, rising from her chair. "Before someone else gets the same idea!"

Chapter XIX

Looking for the Sutter Jewels

OUTSIDE THE WOODS were inky black, for thick clouds covered the moon. Susan Sand and Nanny Maud hurried down the trail toward the path that led up to Raggedrock Ridge. The old crone carried a lantern and trotted beside her companion, muttering to herself, but now and then saying a word or two to Susan. During the trek Susan told Nanny Maud about the night she and Randall Scott followed her to the ridge when she looked for the jewels. The old woman cackled as she listened to Susan's story.

"So you wondered what happened to me!" she chuckled. "Thought I had vanished! Maybe this time they'll be found!"

Once the pair had reached the summit of the ridge, they stopped and looked about. Every so often the moon peeked out from behind the cloud cover and the two figures were silhouetted against the rocks.

"It would be better for us if the moon stayed

hidden," Susan said. "We can be seen too easily, Nanny."

"Yes, the darkness is our protection," she hissed. "Now, let me think. If I was James Benson and I had just been handed the Sutter jewels in that leather pouch, which direction would I go?"

The old crone peered first toward the east, then toward the west, swinging her lantern back and forth.

"It seems to me, Nanny," offered Susan, "that a person on horseback would have only one choice. The trail leads around those rocks and back down the other side."

"You're right, Susan," Nanny Maud agreed. "He would have to circle the boulders over there and then head on down. If the earthquake struck just as he reached the turn, he might have been thrown where the trail takes a sudden dip."

Quickly the pair ran over to the spot and Susan gave a little cry.

"Nanny, this is the very same place where I fell into that hole on Sunday when Dr. Coram and Julia Leck tried to frighten me! Yes, there it is!"

Susan directed her light toward a pile of rocks and pointed out the spot where Julia Leck had fallen against her. In the dark, the hole was at first difficult to find, but soon they had located it.

"If I remember correctly, the drop is about eight feet," Susan said, leaning over the edge and peering down into the blackness. "The earth tremor definitely loosened these rocks. I suspect that Dr. Coram found this hole and covered it over, then had Julia Leck push me so that the loose boulders would fall in when I stepped on them.''

''What nice playmates!'' Nanny Maud muttered. ''Susan, it makes sense that those jewels might be down there. Except for the place where Quentin Sutter met his maker, this spot received the most damage from the earthquake. Let's go down!''

''There are footholes all along the sides,'' Susan replied, flashing her light back and forth. ''But let me go, Nanny. You might get hurt.''

''Ha-ha-ha,'' the old woman cried, almost doubling over with laughter. ''You think I'm going to stand around up here while you have all the fun! Those jewels belong to Penelope, and I'm going to find them! Just give me a hand over the edge and I'll reach the bottom before you do!''

Nanny Maud's spirit amazed Susan Sand. The old crone hung the lantern in the crook of her arm, swung her short legs over the edge, and grabbing on to Susan's hand, turned herself about and started to climb down. Soon she reached the bottom and called up to her companion.

''Nothing to it!'' she cried, cackling.

In a few moments, Susan stood next to her and flashed her light over the sides.

''Nanny, there's a tunnel!'' she exclaimed jubilantly. ''I wonder if it is wide enough to squeeze through?''

Getting down on all fours, Susan stuck her head into the opening. By careful maneuvering, she was able to work her shoulders and squeeze the rest of her body through.

"Nanny, it widens out," Susan called back. "There must be cracks all along this tunnel where the earthquake damaged the rocks."

"We better not have another tremor," the old woman replied, chuckling. "We'd be in a pretty spot!"

Nanny Maud followed Susan through the opening and held up her lantern.

"I can almost stand up," she said, rising to a crouching position. "But I don't see the jewels!"

Slowly the pair searched every inch of the beginning of the tunnel, but they found no leather bag.

"If James Benson rode this way and a crack opened, those jewels could be anywhere along this tunnel," Susan reasoned. "Nanny, we have to follow it to the end or we'll never be satisfied."

"Then what are you waiting for?" she asked. "I'm right behind you!"

Susan, unable to stand erect, started to crawl along the tunnel. She found it difficult to make headway, for the ground was very rocky and she had to be extremely careful with the flashlight.

"If I drop this and it breaks on these rocks, at least we have the lantern," she thought.

The tunnel was extremely irregular and narrowed at one point so that it seemed impossible to continue. Susan became stuck and only a push from Nanny Maud got her through. The old woman was so small that she had no difficulty, and the two went on, creeping on their hands and knees.

Susan glanced at her watch and was amazed to see that they had been in the tunnel for almost an hour.

"We can't have traveled very far," she surmised. "But the going is so slow it seems like miles! Perhaps we are being very foolish. Our chances of finding those jewels appear to be dimming every minute."

"Don't you get discouraged," said Nanny Maud, sensing Susan's state of mind. "The jewels have to be here and we're going to find them!"

"I am beginning to wonder if perhaps James Benson managed to escape the earthquake," Susan admitted. "Nanny, if he was an expert rider and he got away from this spot immediately, he may have ridden off with the jewels and be living on them right now!"

"Of course, that could be," the old woman agreed, setting her lantern on the ground and peering into Susan's face. "But I happen to know that Benson was a terrible horseman and afraid of just about everything except becoming rich. He only rode horseback when he was forced to."

"Then maybe he came to the ridge on foot," Susan exclaimed.

"He could have, but I don't think so," Nanny replied. "I think that he intended to get away with the jewels as fast as he could and turn the tables on Doris Carver. I distinctly recall that the night I returned to the Sutter Mansion, the horse that Benson usually rode, when he did ride, was missing from the stables. No, Susan Sand, he rode up here and dropped those jewels! I'm convinced of it!"

"I hope you are right, Nanny," Susan replied, continuing on down the tunnel. "Oh, I think I see a bit of light. There must be another hole in the earth and the moon has come out!"

Ahead a pale patch of light appeared. Susan began to crawl more quickly and soon had reached the spot. Overhead a narrow crack stretched across the tunnel and Susan could see the moon shining brightly. Flashing her light about, she gave a loud cry as she spotted a small, dark lump over to one side of the cave.

"Nanny, are my eyes deceiving me, or is that a leather pouch?"

Nanny Maud rushed over to the bag and picked it up. Nervously her thin, gnarled fingers tried to open the drawstring, but the lack of the tip of her left forefinger prevented her from doing so.

"Drat this finger!" she lamented, handing the bag to Susan. "Susan, I think we've found them! Just feel those hard pieces in that pouch!"

Susan took the bag and tried to loosen the leather string, but it was stiff with dirt and age. At that moment there was a sound overhead.

"Footsteps!" Susan whispered.

"Someone must have seen us!" Nanny Maud gasped.

Susan put her finger to her lips and shrank back against the side of the tunnel. The footsteps stopped and then started again. All at once a light appeared through the crack that ran along the top of the passageway. Someone was looking directly into the tunnel, trying to seek them out!

Chapter XX

Penelope

"SUSAN? Susan Sand?" called a small voice. "It's Penelope. Are you down there?"

"Penelope!" replied Susan.

"Yes. I saw you with the old woman. Susan, you're looking for the jewels, aren't you?"

"Penelope, don't say anything else," Susan cautioned. "Stay there and we'll come out."

"I had to talk to you," the girl replied, heedless of Susan's words. "Something has happened."

"We can talk later," Susan told her, looking up as Penelope peered through the crack in the earth. "Right now, Nanny Maud and I must get out of this tunnel. Go to the hole where we entered. Do you know where it is?"

"Yes, I saw you go down into it. I'll go there and wait."

Susan Sand and Nanny Maud made their way carefully back through the tunnel, the Sutter jewels safely tucked in the pocket of Susan's jacket.

"What is she doing up here at this hour?"

Nanny Maud anxiously asked. "She sounded upset. What could have happened?"

"I am afraid that Penelope is beginning to discover the truth about her stepfather," Susan surmised. "Think of how upset he would be, Nanny, when he and Julia Leck found out you had escaped. He can't keep his duplicity from Penelope forever!"

"The poor thing!" Nanny Maud exclaimed. "And to think that it's all my fault! She should have been living with Arthur Sutter all these years. Oh, dear, oh, dear!"

"Nanny, please don't blame yourself. Right now we must think of how to catch Dr. Coram and turn him over to the authorities. I'm certain that when Mr. Sutter and Penelope learn the truth, they will understand what a difficult position you have been in."

"I did it all for Christopher," the old crone moaned. "But then it led to his son and then to Penelope. If only that Dudley Coram hadn't adopted her, everything would have turned out all right."

"It still will turn out all right," Susan assured her as they continued to crawl back to the entrance. "Arthur Sutter will be overjoyed to find that Penelope is his heir, and that the jewels have been found. I couldn't have found the jewels without you, Nanny."

"Oh, I hope you are right, Susan," she replied. "I've lived hiding the truth for so long, I'm afraid of what people will think, especially Mr. Sutter."

"It all happened so long ago, I am certain he will forgive you," Susan answered. "You took Christopher because no one else cared for him the way you did. That's what you will tell Mr. Sutter—the truth, Nanny."

When they reached the end of the tunnel and squeezed through the hole into the cave, Penelope was looking down from above, her flashlight balanced on the rim of the crevice. Nanny Maud got a foothold on a large rock and started to climb up, Susan close behind her. As the old woman reached the edge, Penelope helped her over.

"Penelope, do you know who I am?" the old woman asked.

"Yes, Nanny, I do," the girl answered, taking her in her arms.

"Penelope, what's happened?" Susan asked.

"Julia Leck came to the house a short time ago," the girl explained. "She was very upset and rushed into my father's consulting room. I was supposed to be in bed, but I heard her voice and I was curious. I've been suspicious for a long time that something was wrong. I listened to their conversation."

"What did they say, child?" Nanny Maud queried.

"They talked about you, Nanny, and how you had escaped," Penelope answered. "At first I didn't know what they were talking about, but then they said something about you and Christopher Sutter and that you were his Nanny many years ago."

"Penelope, this is a dangerous place to talk," Susan cautioned. "We must go somewhere so that we can't be seen."

"Let's go to the stables," Penelope suggested. "No one will find us there, and the horses know me so they won't be disturbed by our presence."

"How did you find us?" Susan asked as the trio started down the path from Raggedrock Ridge.

"I was so upset by what I heard, I ran from the house," Penelope answered. "I saw you up on the ridge. Susan, is it true? Am I really a Sutter?"

"Did you hear Dr. Coram and Julia Leck say that?"

"Yes," replied Penelope, her voice tight with emotion. "Is it true?"

"Yes, child, it is true," Nanny Maud answered. "You are the granddaughter of Christopher Sutter."

"But why would father keep that from me all these years?" the girl wondered. "If he knew, why didn't he tell me? And why did they kidnap you, Nanny?"

"They kidnapped me because I know who you are," Nanny Maud replied kindly. "And they thought I knew where the jewels were."

"I heard Julia Leck say something about the jewels," Penelope stated.

"Hurry, Penelope," Susan warned. "Let's get

to the stables before we are seen. I have the Sutter jewels in my pocket!''

The moon suddenly emerged from behind the clouds as the three reached the protection of the Dudley stables. Penelope talked comfortingly to the horses and prevented them from making any disturbance. Taking a lantern from the wall, she lit it and stood looking at Susan and Nanny Maud, her expression puzzled and disturbed.

''Then I really and truly am Penelope Sutter,'' she said simply.

''Yes, Penelope,'' Susan answered. ''Nanny Maud left you on Arthur Sutter's doorstep fifteen years ago because she wanted you to be brought up as a Sutter. Your grandfather was killed in World War Two and your parents in an accident when you were only ten months old. Dr. Coram and Miss Leck must have found you with the note Nanny left explaining who you were, and Dr. Coram adopted you with the hopes of getting the Sutter money someday.''

''Oh, how terrible!'' the girl gasped, sinking down onto a pile of hay. ''I always thought that father was secretive about my past, but I kept telling myself that no one knew who I was. And all the time he kept the truth from me!''

Penelope threw herself over onto her face and started to sob.

''Now, now, child,'' said Nanny Maud, taking the girl by the shoulders and cooing gently. ''Just think how you are a Sutter and how Arthur Sutter is your cousin. Imagine how happy he will be to learn that he has an heir, and a pretty one at that!"

"Oh, Nanny," Penelope cried, throwing herself into the old woman's arms. "My home has been Dudley House and Dr. Coram my father! How can I ever face him again? And that Julia Leck! I never liked her, and now I find out that she and Father are kidnappers!"

"Penelope," said Susan, taking the girl's hand. "You must think of Arthur Sutter and Miss Greenway. Miss Greenway has been good to you, hasn't she?"

"She's been like a mother," Penelope admitted, sitting up and wiping her eyes with a handkerchief. "In recent years I have been afraid of Father, and Miss Greenway has protected me from him. He has terrible bursts of anger and he's been so nervous, especially in the last few days. Oh, what am I going to do?"

"The truth has to come out," Susan said. "Penelope, you must face the fact that your father and Miss Leck have committed a criminal act. They will certainly go to jail."

"Then what's going to happen to me?" Penelope cried. "Where will I go?"

"Arthur Sutter is your cousin, Penelope," Nanny Maud reminded her. "Why, you will be living at the Sutter Mansion with servants and all the things you have always wanted!"

"I have always cared for Mr. Sutter," Penelope said. "He and I have a great deal in common.

We've had some nice talks and he seems to be fond of me."

"I know he thinks highly of you," Susan answered. "He told me so himself."

"What are you going to do, Susan?" Penelope asked. "Go to the police?"

"Yes, Penelope, but I must find Professor Scott and Brian Lorenzo. Do you know where they are?"

"They were so concerned over where you had gone that they went into Foxboro. Professor Scott said something about visiting Miss Bingham at the Wayside Orphanage."

"I told Randall that I intended to visit Miss Bingham," Susan explained. "Nanny, we must get you to a safe place."

"I know!" Penelope exclaimed. "Why not go up to the Tower Room, Nanny? You will be safe there and Father would never think of looking for you in his own house!"

"What a good idea!" Susan agreed.

"But how am I to get up there?" Nanny Maud questioned. "What if Dr. Coram sees me?"

"We have to think of a way to get you inside secretly," Susan mused. "Penelope, where is your father right now?"

"He was still in his consulting room with Miss Leck," she replied. "I think that Miss Leck was about to leave."

"I'd better go back to my cottage," said Nanny Maud.

"No, Nanny!" said Susan. "I am going to get you into Dudley House through Marge's window!"

"Through Marge's window!" Penelope cried.

"Yes! That's the very way I got back in the night I was locked in the basement. Hurry, we'll creep up to the house and tap on the pane. It's the safest way!"

Chapter XXI

In the Tower Room

THE CLOUDS HAD DISPERSED and the night sky was brightly lit by a full moon. Susan Sand, Nanny Maud, and Penelope Sutter hurried from the stables toward Dudley House, their running figures clearly etched out in the white moonlight. From a distance, the house looked dark and foreboding. Only one lamp lit a front window.

"Julia Leck is gone," Penelope whispered. "I don't see her car."

"Hurry!" Susan urged. "Dr. Coram mustn't see us!"

When the trio reached Marge's window, Susan tapped lightly on the pane and called softly through the partially open sash.

"Marge, it's Susan," she said. "I have Nanny Maud with me."

"Sue!" came back a startled voice. "Nanny Maud? What do you mean?"

The redhead soon appeared, hobbling across the room on her crutches. She opened the window wide and Penelope and Susan helped Nanny Maud over the sill and climbed in after her.

"There is no time to explain," Susan said in a hushed voice. "Marge, we found the Sutter jewels! I have them in my pocket!"

"What! The jewels! Penelope! Where have you been?"

Briefly, Susan explained what had occurred.

"We've been so worried, Sue," Marge said, looking at Nanny Maud curiously. "Brian and Randall are at the orphanage or maybe at the police station."

Susan pulled the bag of jewels from her pocket and held it up.

"We found these up on the ridge," she stated, describing the tunnel. "Marge, is Dr. Coram still up?"

"I don't know," she replied. "Miss Leck left about fifteen minutes ago. What a state she was in! Miss Greenway is in the living room. I couldn't sleep, and she and I have been talking."

"Marge, Penelope and I have decided to hide Nanny Maud in the Tower Room," Susan revealed. "I think the wisest thing for us to do is to enter normally through the front door. I'll tell Miss Greenway that I became lost in the woods and that Penelope came looking for me. While we divert her attention, you show Nanny where the back stairs are so she can get up to the Tower Room."

"What if Dr. Coram should see us?" Marge

asked, an expression of deep concern spreading over her freckled face.

"You should be able to get Nanny to the stairs, Marge," Penelope stated. "If he is still in his consulting room, he will never hear anything."

"I hope you're right," she said. "What will I say if we are caught?"

"Think positively," Susan replied, smiling at her friend. "Penelope, after we enter by the front door, I'll go on up to my room so as not to arouse suspicion."

"And I'll bring Miss Greenway to the study," Penelope added. "Then I'll come for you, Marge, once Nanny is safely upstairs. I want to talk to both you and Miss Greenway."

Susan and Penelope climbed back outside and closed the window halfway. Nanny Maud looked worried and frightened as her two friends disappeared around the corner of the house.

"I hope this is going to work," Penelope whispered apprehensively. "If Father ever catches them, I don't know what will happen!"

"If only Randall and Brian were here," Susan replied.

The pair approached the front door and Penelope pulled out her key. As she turned it in the lock and opened the door, Miss Greenway ran toward them.

"Penelope!" she cried. "Where have you been? I've looked all over the house. And Susan! What's happened?"

"Sssh, we're fine," said Penelope consolingly. "Where's Father?"

"I don't know," Miss Greenway replied. "He was talking to Julia in the consulting room, but she left a short time ago. Pen, what is going on?"

"Let's go into the study," the girl replied, taking the woman's hand. "I must talk to you, but I am so afraid that Father will hear us."

"Susan, where were you all this time?"

"I was lost in the woods," Susan replied. "I went to do some research for my book and I broke my compass. Fortunately, Penelope thought of what might have happened so she came looking for me."

"Oh, Penelope! I know you were worried about Susan, but you could have become lost, too!"

"Please, Miss Greenway," the girl said. "Everything is all right now. Let's go into the study. Susan wants to go to her room and get some sleep."

The housekeeper followed Penelope to the study and Susan started toward the stairs that led up to the Tower Room. The big house was silent and there was no sign of Dr. Coram. Down the hall she could see the door of his consulting room but no light appeared underneath the sill. Quietly, Susan began to ascend the stairs, trying to avoid the places that she knew squeaked.

Halfway up to the first landing, there was a faint noise and Susan shrank back against the wall, scarcely able to breathe. For a seemingly

endless period of time she waited, expecting Dr.
Coram to appear at the bottom of the staircase.
Suddenly there was a soft mewing sound and a
small, furry body darted out from the shadows.

"Icky!" Susan gasped. "Oh, Icky!"

Picking up her pet, Susan continued the ascent, her heart pounding violently against her
ribs. Reaching the door of the Tower Room, she
silently turned the knob and slipped quickly into
the chamber.

"Nanny?" she called softly, "why didn't you
turn on the light?"

Susan looked about but there was no sign of
the old woman. The moon shone brightly
through the large, round windows, and Raggedrock Ridge loomed clearly in the distance.

"Perhaps Marge was afraid to take the chance
of getting her to the stairs," she told herself, turning on a light. "Oh, I hope nothing has happened!"

Susan took the Sutter jewels out of the pocket
of her jacket and placed the pouch on the bed.

"If only I could open this bag, Icky!" she lamented, trying to loosen the drawstring that held
the pouch securely fastened. "Eighty years of
dirt and damp have practically cemented it
closed!"

Susan worked diligently on the leather thong,
not wanting to cut it with scissors, for she considered the bag an heirloom and was reluctant to
damage it in any way. The leather was beginning
to crack in several places and the thong started to

split whenever she attempted to draw it through the small holes around the top. After several minutes of struggling with the bag, Susan replaced it on the counterpane.

"What could have happened to Nanny Maud?" she asked herself, her concern mounting. "She should be up here by now."

Susan crossed to the door and quietly opened it. Looking into the darkness, she contemplated returning downstairs but rejected the idea as too dangerous.

"If I ever met Dr. Coram, he would wonder why I was up at this hour, and I would have to answer a lot of difficult questions. Nanny Maud, where are you?"

Susan closed the door and returned to the bed. Sitting down next to Icky and picking up the bag of jewels, she began to work at the leather drawstring again. All at once it loosened and the bag opened!

"Oh, look at these jewels!" she exclaimed, spilling them out onto the bed. "Why there must be dozens of them! How beautiful they are!"

Suddenly there was a sound from the direction of the balcony. Susan looked up, startled, for the door to the outside was opening! Ikhnaton jumped to his feet, his fur bristling, and spit.

"Dr. Coram!" Susan cried as the bulky figure of the doctor entered the room, a gun in his hand.

"Yes, Susan Sand, Dr. Coram," he replied, stroking his moustache and looking excitedly at the jewels that lay scattered on the bed. "So you were lost in the woods? I think not. You very kindly found the Sutter jewels for me! Now, if you will just hand them over, I won't be forced to use this revolver!"

Chapter XXII

A Halloween Surprise

"I AM SURPRISED that you would resort to such crude methods, Doctor," replied Susan Sand, rising to her feet and looking steadily into Dr. Coram's face. "Now that you have been found out, you act like a common criminal."

"If it weren't for you, Susan Sand, I would be getting all the Sutter money," the doctor retorted, his voice menacing and his eyes glittering with anger. "The Sutter jewels are an unexpected recompense for all your meddling! Hand them over!"

Slowly Susan started to gather the scattered gems together, putting them into the pouch one by one. Her motions were careful and deliberate as she coolly dropped each sparkling jewel into the bag.

"They are beautiful, aren't they, Doctor?" she mused, holding up an especially large and gleaming ruby. "It seems to me that this one

174

would look extremely nice on Penelope, as a pendant, perhaps.''

"Stop stalling!" Dr. Coram warned, crossing over to within several feet of the bed. "Give me those jewels, now!"

"What do you intend to do once you have them?" Susan asked, putting the last stone into the bag and tightening the thong. "Escape from your own home and take an assumed name?"

With great fury, Dr. Coram lunged forward and grabbed the leather pouch from Susan's hand. Icky flew from the bed and dove underneath it, his tail flicking and low growls issuing from his throat.

"Your cat is not much protection," Dr. Coram taunted.

"If it weren't for Icky, I never would have learned about the paper identifying Penelope," Susan rejoined, the corners of her mouth turning up mockingly. "He gave me the most important clue of all."

"A lot of good your clues will do you now," the doctor replied derisively, fingering his revolver.

At that moment there was a slight movement behind Dr. Coram. The closet door was slowly opening! Susan tried not to show her amazement for Nanny Maud emerged and began to creep up behind the doctor as he held his weapon leveled on Susan! The old crone came steadily forward, silently, until she was barely two feet from him.

Dr. Coram was apparently unaware of her presence, for he did not turn his head, so intent was he on the bag of jewels in his hand.

"So, Dudley Coram, you're nothing but a thug!" Nanny Maud cried, causing the doctor to spin around. Instantly, Susan knocked the revolver from his hand and retrieved the bag of gems. The gun landed on the edge of the rug and then bounded off and slid under the bed.

"Nanny!" Susan exclaimed. "You've been in the closet all this time!"

Before the old woman could answer, there were pounding footsteps on the stairs, and Randall Scott, Brian Lorenzo, and several burly policemen burst into the room. Penelope and Miss Greenway were right behind them, Penelope's face gray with fear and the housekeeper's expression one of astonishment.

"Father!" cried Penelope, pushing her way past the group and running over to Dr. Coram.

"I'm not your father," he replied coldly, brushing by her into the arms of the waiting authorities. "I found you on Arthur Sutter's doorstep."

"Sue, are you all right?" Professor Scott anxiously asked.

"Everything is fine, Randall," Susan replied, putting her arm around Nanny Maud. "Nanny had hidden in the closet, and between us we managed to disarm Dr. Coram!"

"I came up here right away," Nanny Maud explained, grinning. "But no sooner had I sat down than I heard footsteps. I knew they weren't yours, Susan, so I hid in the closet. Then I heard you come in but I was afraid that whoever had entered before you, might see me if I opened the door. So I just waited."

"You did the wise thing, Nanny," Susan said. "He might have had time to escape if it weren't for your presence of mind."

"Julia Leck has been arrested," said Brian.

"Then it's all over," added Penelope, sinking down on the bed and putting her face in her hands.

"No, Penelope, it's just beginning for you," Susan replied, sitting down next to her. "You are Penelope Sutter. Think of what that will mean for the rest of your life!"

Two large pumpkins, skillfully carved into grinning faces, lit up the front windows of Dudley House with the soft glow of candlelight. Within the house a laughing group of people were gathered together in the living room, which had been decorated with orange and black streamers, dancing skeletons, flying witches, and menacing bats.

"If this Halloween party hadn't been your idea, Penelope, it would have been mine," said Marge Halloran, relaxing in a comfortable chair by the fire. "I love parties!"

"Especially when you don't have to do the work!" chided Brian Lorenzo, climbing down from a ladder near the window where he had just hung the last decoration, a huge black bat.

"How can I work with a sprained ankle, silly!" she rejoined, munching on a cupcake.

"Don't tease her so much," said Penelope, sitting between Arthur Sutter and Esther Greenway on the couch. "You're merciless!"

Suddenly two large, furry animals raced through the room and up the stairs.

"Am I mistaken, or was that two cats?" Arthur Sutter asked, looking after the two creatures.

Penelope squealed gaily.

"That was Icky and Fussy," she explained. "Fussy has become my cat since Julia Leck is unable to take care of him!"

"What a lucky cat!" the millionaire rejoined, pulling the girl toward him and kissing her on the cheek.

"It seems that cats have had a great deal to do with this case," added Miss Bingham from her seat by the window. "Casper was very valuable that day at the orphanage, wasn't he, Susan?"

"He certainly was," the raven-haired sleuth replied. "He proved that the piece of paper identifying Penelope had been in Julia Leck's canister. That note was our most important clue."

Nanny Maud, seated on the other side of the fire from Marge, was silently sipping a cup of tea. She was dressed in a black satin outfit, very old and worn, and with her sharp nose and black eyes, she looked somewhat like a Halloween witch herself.

"Nanny is going to continue to live in the cottage in the woods," Penelope revealed.

"I intend to have the place redone just for you, Nanny," Arthur Sutter said, "exactly the way you want it."

"I don't deserve it," she answered shyly. "You have all been very kind."

"Of course you deserve it," Esther Greenway rejoined. "Nanny, without you Penelope may never have come into her inheritance."

"That was brave, the way you confronted Dr. Coram," added Susan.

"But it was you who found the jewels," Nanny replied.

"With your help, Nanny," Susan reminded her.

Randall Scott came over to Susan Sand and put his arm around her waist.

"Susan is a clever and wonderful girl," he said simply. "Julia Leck found that out to her detriment!"

"How did you ever think of looking for the jewels in that tunnel?" George Reger asked.

"It was like solving a riddle," Susan answered, adjusting her glasses. "Since Quentin Sutter didn't drop them, we reasoned they must have been in James Benson's possession by the time the earthquake happened. By following the path of Benson's horse, Nanny and I solved the mystery between us!"

"Here is another mystery that I am going to unsolve," Arthur Sutter announced. "Esther Greenway and I are to be married, and she has picked one of the Sutter jewels for her engagement ring."

Cries of delight echoed around the room, and a bottle of champagne was brought in to celebrate the event.

"And I am going to the Sutter Mansion to live," Penelope divulged.

"Then what will become of Dudley House?" Marge blurted.

"Since I own all this property and the house as well, I shall rent it," Arthur Sutter answered. "Dudley Coram had leased the house and often didn't come through with the payments! And now that the jewels have been found, I will sell some of them and redecorate the mansion. My financial position hasn't been as sound as most people think! Finding those jewels will enable me to give Penelope and Esther all they deserve!"

"I have one final surprise," Susan Sand announced, picking up a large candle and placing it on a plate. "I found this candle inside an old lantern in the Dudley stables. Nanny, I want you to light it."

"You want me to light the candle," said Nanny Maud, a puzzled expression on her wrinkled features. "Whatever for?"

"Come over here, Nanny, and put this match to the wick," Susan urged.

Nanny Maud rose from her chair and went over to where the fat candle reposed in the saucer. Striking the match, she lit the wick and watched as it started to burn. Slowly the wax began to melt. Nanny looked up at Susan Sand and then back at the candle.

"Oh, look!" cried Penelope. "There's something in the top!"

At that moment an object dropped to the table, and Nanny Maud picked it up, an expression of wonderment on her face.

"Christopher's baby ring!" she exclaimed, wiping off the wax with the hem of her skirt. "It's been in the candle all this time!"

"But how did it get there?" Marge queried, hobbling across to the table on her crutches.

"Remember how we talked about Doris Carver?" Susan replied. "She was making candles in the stables the day of the earthquake. Apparently when James Benson brought the baby Christopher to her, she noticed the ring and broke it off the chain because she was unable to undo the catch. Then she didn't know where to hide it, for she wanted it for herself, so she pushed it into the soft wax in this candle that she had just made."

"Whatever made you think of it, Sue?" Professor Scott inquired.

"The day we got the horses to ride up to

Raggedrock Ridge, I saw the lantern lying in the corner of the stables," she replied. "Then when Nanny Maud told me about the ring and the fact that Doris made the candles, I decided she may very well have used one of the candles as a hiding place. And I was right!"

Nanny Maud pulled the small gold chain which Susan had returned to her from her bag and placed the tiny ring to the spot where it had been broken off.

"It fits exactly," she announced.

"The ring is yours, Nanny," Arthur Sutter told her.

"Oh, thank you, Mr. Sutter," she murmured, tears running down her cheeks. "I can't think of anything else that could mean so much to me."

"I have one final surprise," said the millionaire, reaching into his pocket and pulling out a little black box. "Susan, this is for you. It's my material payment for all you have done for us."

Susan took the box and opened it.

"A black pearl!" she gasped. "Mr. Sutter, what a marvelous gift!"

"It's the least I can do," Arthur Sutter replied. "Except perhaps to give Icky a lifetime supply of shrimp and caviar!"

At that moment Icky and Fussy flew down the stairs and through the room.

"Those two cats are going to be friends for life!" said Susan, laughing.

"There is nothing better than good friends,"

added Penelope. "Susan Sand, you've turned out to be the best friend of all!"

Friendship again plays an important role in Susan's next case, *The Phantom of Featherford Falls,* when she helps an Indian boy solve an age-old mystery.

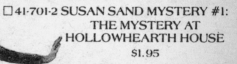